The Strange Metamorphosis
Of Zachary Warren

Joe Randazzo

A Sprezzatura Book
From New Renaissance Press

Sprezzatura Books
New Renaissance Press
8 Woodside Drive
South Burlington, VT 05403

ISBN 978-0-9851615-0-7

Library of Congress Control Number
2012902356

This book is a work of fiction. Character names and incidents in the plot are products of the author's imagination. Any resemblance to actual events or persons, living or dead, is entirely coincidental.

Author's photograph: Chris Koch

For Rita Randazzo, A highly flammable intoxicant

Also by Joe Randazzo

Poetry
Coffee House
His/Hers: Mars and Venus Write Poetry
(with Rita Randazzo)

Novels
Screen
Van Eyck's Secret
See Dick Run: A Grownup's Picture Book
Walking Man
AfterWorld

Photodocumentary
Going With the Wind: Carolina in My Mind

Chapter One

"Aw Dad, do I have to? Mom, why can't I watch the dancing?" Ethan whines.

"Okay, you can stay up, but you must go to bed right after the show."

"Oh great, Daphne! I say he should go to bed, and you allow him to stay up and watch Dancing with the Degenerates. He has school tomorrow, for Christ's sake. This garbage isn't over until eleven. You let him sit there on your lap while he watches these talentless buffoons gyrate in our faces."

"Not now, Zachary. We'll discuss this later."

"Oh sure. As soon as logic intervenes, you want to discuss it later."

"Not in front of the children, Zachary."

For the next hour, the Warren family, Dr. Zachary, age thirty-six, his wife Daphne, thirty-four, their son Ethan, six, and their daughter Emma, thirteen, watch their four-by-six-foot flat panel TV in relative silence, broken only by Ethan, who claps whenever a dancer twirls his partner high in the air.

"I suppose it's now time for the two of you to go into your bedroom for another round of bickering. That's real private, like we can't hear every word you say," Emma says with a bored cadence in her voice. "I thought for a second we might go an entire day without your usual antics. I have soccer practice in the morning, so don't keep me awake."

"Dad, can you read me a story before I go to bed?"

"It's too late, Ethan, and I have to get up to go to work in the morning, same as you."

"Would it kill you to read him a story, Zachary? You don't have to read War and Stinking Peace, just something of interest to make him sleep better."

"Fine, Daphne, fine." He gives her a hateful look as he walks back to Ethan's bedroom at the opposite end of the long, walnut-paneled hall. Zachary doesn't see Daphne, who discreetly follows them.

"Here's your story, Ethan. A man was born at a very early age, in a very faraway place. He lived a very ordinary life, and died at a very old age, in an even further away place. End of story. Now go to sleep."

"What was that supposed to be?" Daphne bursts into Ethan's room.

"That's the new short fiction. It's all the rage, you know."

"Very funny, Zachary. Why don't you read him one of these?" She hands him the collected stories of Edward Randall, Zachary's favorite author.

He snatches the book from Daphne and chooses the seventh story. He reads to Ethan.

PowZak

Louise awakened in a frenzy, said she had a dream about a magic potion that could do many wondrous things. Since the clock said 5:45 a.m. on a Saturday morning, I wasn't very enthusiastic or supportive. I believe I muttered something unkind, turned over, placed the comforter over my cold left ear, and tried to go back to sleep.

Sleep would be impossible. She was up and in the kitchen. The cacophony commenced: water running, pots crashing, laughter, cursing, bubbling and gurgling sounds, and the whirring of electric appliances. She went out to the shed in the cold drizzle and came back with a can of WD-40, a can of brake fluid, some clear polyurethane paint, dried sage, mushrooms, and some other weird plants in a clear plastic bag.

I asked her what she was doing, and she screamed, "Ralph, get out of my kitchen! Can't you see I'm working on something important?" I asked her when she would fix breakfast, but she didn't even lift her head up to answer.

This went on all morning. At noon, I left to look at used pickup trucks, since we were soon to buy one, and stopped off at the hamburger place for some lunch. I'd been home about half an hour when she came out of the kitchen at 2:00 and handed me an eight-ounce bottle of amber-colored liquid. The substance was smoking like dry ice exposed to the air, and it felt just slightly warm to the touch. It had a very pleasant fragrance, like the forest after a spring rain. "What is it?" I asked.

"PowZak," she replied.

"Well, what the hell is PowZak?" I asked impatiently. "What's in it?"

"Just mix a few drops of it with whatever else you are using, and it will do most anything," she replied.

I asked her to give me some examples of what it could do, and this is what she told me. "Add a few drops to a glass of water, and it will quench your thirst. Add a few drops to paint, and you can redo the ceiling. Add a few drops to your aftershave lotion, and you will smell nice. Add a few drops to plant food, and the philodendron will grow."

"Wait a minute, wait a minute," I snapped. "Did it ever occur to your tiny brain that all these chemicals would work just fine without your PowZak?"

She just smiled, shrugged her shoulders, and told me to try using it on something. Off she went to her Saturday women's group, where they make clay goddess figures, beat on their doumbeks and bodhrans, do weird chanting, and read improbable feminist literature. I sat there holding this amber-colored liquid. We had been invited to dinner by some friends, so I went to the bathroom to shave. I started laughing when I thought of what she had done. I stared into the mirror at my nearly bald head and chuckled to myself. *I'll get some PowZak and rub it on my head. No more baldness, no more gray hair, yuk yuk. I'll also rub some on my stomach, and maybe my beer slope will disappear. I know, I'll rub some on my muscles and other parts, and maybe they'll get bigger, hee hee.*

So I went into the kitchen and grabbed the bottle and rubbed it on. I finished shaving and put on some music. I walked into the bedroom to get dressed and noticed that my belt was too big and my underwear was too small. I felt the top of my head and ran into the bathroom. There I was, in the mirror with a full head of black hair, no more gut, big biceps and a ten-inch gertoodle, on soft.

"Zachary this isn't appropriate for a six-year-old boy," Daphne whispers angrily as she bursts into the child's bedroom. Ethan is asleep, so they return to their bedroom and close the door.

Zachary speaks calmly but emphatically. "Look, Daphne, you let him sit up and watch these morons gyrate. You let him play with his sisters dolls and stuffed animals."

"That story isn't suitable for a child, and you know it."

"Oh, the mention of his ten-inch gertoodle pushed you over the edge, did it? What are you going to tell Ethan when he asks you what that thing between his legs is for? It's to decorate with dolly's clothes. You can wrap a tiny lace scarf around it, and you can paint a happy face on the end of your dick, it you'd like. Or is it his jane? He's a boy, for Christ's sake. He has a penis. You are familiar with that object. I did create our children with it."

"All by yourself, did you? Let me tell you something. Even without your penis, they would still be *my* children."

"Oh, another brilliant statement by the queen of logic! If I fathered two children by a woman other than you, they would still be *my* children. What the hell does that prove?"

Zachary slams the door and carries Randall's book to his study to finish the story. Emma is waiting in the hall with her arms folded. "Do you know what I'm going to do? I'm going to record your fights and post them on Facebook. I think the world should hear what a man with two doctorates, one in Microbiology and the other in Chemical Biology, and a woman with her Masters degree in psychology, of all things, have to say to each other. I might make CDs and sell them at school. That should help our social standing."

"Very funny. Em, I'm sorry we kept you up. Go to sleep, and I promise there will be no more fighting."

«««◊»»»

Zachary closes the door to his study. He turns on his antique Italian wrought-iron floor lamp that has been retrofitted with a special halogen bulb and continues reading Edward Randall's *PowZak*.

...After getting over the shock, I admired myself in the mirror. I also stared at the bottle and wondered what was going on. Louise came home and said that I looked nice but that I'm too preoccupied with my own appearance. I should consider doing more meaningful things with PowZak. When

I asked her what was in it, she smiled and said it was just a recipe her tiny brain had invented, a secret recipe.

I spent all morning Sunday staring at that bottle. I went back and forth to the mirror about fifty times. I guess it's going to take a while for me to get used to my new looks. Wait until my hot secretary Carol sees me. I thought of what else we could do with that liquid. How about rubbing some on the fender of the Chevrolet, which got bashed in the parking lot? Would it straighten out the dents? Was this just the power of suggestion as far as my own body was concerned? Could it really do anything to anything? Was she playing a trick on me? I had to find out.

I rubbed some on the fender and went back inside the house and watched it. I watched and watched until way after sunset, but nothing happened. I turned on the outside floodlight and stayed up until midnight, looking at the front fender of that old Chevrolet. Nothing happened. I went to sleep, and Monday morning when I walked out the side door to leave for work, my neighbor congratulated me on my new car. "That's a neat Jaguar, same color as your old car," he said. "I notice that it also has a dink in the front fender. That should be easy to fix. Where'd you get it?"

I stuttered and said, "PowZak Motors, it's Louise's car, I dunno." He said he liked my new hairpiece and asked me if I was working out. I fumbled for my keys and dropped them in the wet driveway. There were three new keys on it, and the ignition key had a cat emblem. I didn't know what to think. I ran back into the house.

I wasn't going to work today. "God damn it, Louise!" I bellowed. "Are you playing a joke on me? Did you switch cars just to play a joke?" She shrugged her shoulders, and with a wry smile, shook her head no.

"Why are you so predictable?" she asked. "If a genie granted you three wishes, the first two would be a new car and a new boat. The third would probably be long life, or some other last minute, catch-up request."

I protested. "I didn't wish for a new car, only a new fender for the old car."

"Is that the best you can do with PowZak?"

"No way! It wasn't that stuff!" I shouted. "Someone put the Jaguar there! That liquid is a figment of your bullshit imagination. I'm going to really test it this time."

I changed into my jeans and black sweatshirt with Carpe Diem on the front. Much less afraid now, I climbed into the Jag and revved the engine. Seven music discs were in the holder by the player. It was music I don't generally listen to, like *The William Tell Overture* and *The Ride of the Valkyries*. It was all stirring, vibrant music that made me drive too fast and made me feel like I could do anything.

The PowZak was in an unbreakable thermos on the front seat next to me. I rubbed some on the wrinkled fender and walked away from it to test a theory. When I came back two minutes later the fender was perfect. This sneaky shit works, all right, but it doesn't work when it's being watched. I was perspiring heavily. It's also unpredictable, because it didn't fix the fender when the car was first changed from the Chevy to the Jag.

Would PowZak clone money? Could I rub some on fifty-dollar bills and cause them to reproduce? Could I make a stack of copies and turn them into real money? I headed for the bank and ReproCopy. My cellphone wasn't in the Jag, so I stopped at a phone booth to call Carol. We have been seeing each other for four months now, and I knew she would wonder why I wasn't at work. I left the Jag's engine running, shut the door, and quickly pushed the buttons on the phone. After the second ring, I heard the engine revving. I looked up to see two punks with tattooed arms back up and squeal the tires as they fled the parking lot. I ran outside, but it was too late to stop them. I went back inside the phone booth, hung up on Carol, and called Louise to tell her what happened. "Two thieves stole the Jaguar, and the PowZak is on the front seat. Can you make that again? Is that the only bottle?"

"Ralph, you're an idiot," she said, and slammed down the phone. I quickly dialed 911 and described the car. What was the license plate number? I hoped that the Chevy plate was now on the Jag and gave them the number. About thirty minutes later a patrol car showed up with two very bored officers who filled out a report. I knew I couldn't tell them that I had to have the Jaguar back because I wanted the thermos on the front seat. They drove me back to the station, and I waited for several hours, hoping for news.

No news came, so I called a cab and rode home. Louise was out, and I was alone. The phone rang an hour later; it was the police. They had caught the robber, and my Jag was in good shape. I rushed down in another cab and after filling out five more forms got the Jaguar back. I found the thermos in the front seat, but it was empty. Did one of the thieves drink the PowZak? I had to know what happened, so I asked the sergeant where the two men were. I told him I had to talk to them. He refused and said there was only one man, and he was in custody; only his attorney could contact him. I begged him for information.

"Did he seem different or peculiar?" I pleaded. He told me the guy looked like a normal sleazebag to him. I said "What about the other man? I told you there were two men."

"Look pal," the sergeant said impatiently, "we're trying to find this guy. You got your car back, so relax." I had to think quickly, so I told him a lie. "Listen Sarge, I was doing a botany experiment. There was a poison in that thermos that if it's drunk will cause death about twenty-four hours later unless I give the antidote."

"Why didn't you say so in the first place!" the sergeant shouted. "Well, why break our necks finding him?" he said. "By this time tomorrow, he'll be dead. I won't have to go to court on my day off, har har. Okay, okay, I'll add these facts to the report. We'll try to find this poor baby."

I went back to the Jaguar. Shaken and upset, I was driving sixty-five in a thirty-five mile school zone. I suddenly felt the car slow down. The acceleration was more like my old Chevy. My god! It *was* the old Chevy! The car had changed back again, and my CD player had on rap music that I never listen to. I almost lost control of the car, so I pulled off the road. I looked in the rearview mirror and saw a gold earring in my right ear, and noticed that I had tattoos on my hands and arms. My face was the same as the punk at the police station who stole the Jag.

I raced back to my house as fast as I could. As I drove up the street, the engine conked out dead, and I rolled to a stop in front of our neighbor's yard. Louise and the other tattooed punk raced out of the driveway in a new Jaguar, pulling a small U-haul trailer. They waved and sped away.

《《《〈〉》》》

Zachary closes the book and muses about *PowZak*. which seemed to have been named after him. What would *he* do if he developed such a wonder drug? He turns out his floor lamp and returns to their bedroom. Daphne is waiting up for him. This time they speak barely above a whisper, but their

12

volume increases steadily as their discussion becomes more heated.

"What are you doing, Daphne? You're teaching Ethan to think like a pussy, and you're raising Emma to be a storm trooper. She works out with weights and wants to join the boys' soccer team because she's stronger and faster than they are."

"What's wrong with that? She's a tough girl. Why shouldn't she be allowed to....."

"I don't want to hear any more gender neutral crap, Daphne. Your daffy mother is its chief proponent, after she raised you normally, of course. The two of you go on and on about how a child should choose his gender. I've got news for you, woman, it doesn't work that way."

"Stereotypes are made to be broken," Daphne says. "Your analytical mind can't think outside the box."

"Is that so? Let me tell you something, woman. You are going to raise an entire generation of kids who won't know which bathroom to use. I can see it now in the elementary schools: boys, girls, and gender neutral. They will be the first generation that tries to fuck itself."

"You're sick!" Daphne shouts. "You talk about your penis, yet you haven't come near me for three months. What good is that thing?" Daphne cries. "I insist we see a marriage counselor."

"Oh great, a marriage counselor, just like your mother. Perhaps we should just sit in her living room, and she can analyze our relationship from her gender neutral perspective. Your gender neutral father can also be present."

"Go ahead, insult my parents, at least I know who mine are," Daphne sobs. "You don't love me anymore. All we ever do is fight. My mother was right. We need to see a marriage counselor right away."

Chapter Two

Drs. Mitchell and Florence Sidthern met at Yale, where they were both studying psychology. They married ten years ago and started their own practice. They are the personal friends of Mildred Pettersen, Daphne's mother. They do not counsel individuals, only couples. They have a highly unusual, and probably illegal, method of learning about the couples they are treating. The Sidtherns believe what couples say to each other in unguarded moments, in the waiting room when they think they are alone, reveals much about their problems. It usually takes many months of therapy before the same information is uncovered. They have a hidden camera with a wide-angle lens and microphone in the false ceiling. They always make the couple being treated wait for twenty minutes before they invite them in. After therapy, their patients leave by the back door. There is usually a couple being recorded in the waiting room while another is being treated in the therapy room. They review the videos after the couples leave, study their body language and speech, and transcribe important facts into their notes. They then destroy the videos. If anyone discovers the camera, they are prepared to say that it's a security precaution and potential evidence in cases of domestic violence.

Zachary and Daphne Warren are sitting in the waiting room in total silence. He is reading the July issue of *Popular Mechanics*, and she is reading the August issue of *People*. Their glances meet only once, and then they both quickly look back down at their magazines.

Dr. Florence Sidthern walks into the waiting room and welcomes them. "Hello Daphne, it's so good to see you, and you must be Zachary. I've heard a lot about you from the Pettersens. They really think the world of you, and I'm so glad you are going to give us the honor of helping you through this little rough spot."

The doctor continued talking as they walked into the therapy room. Mitchell shook hands with both of them and invited them to sit anywhere they liked. There were two soft beanbag chairs, an Adirondack chair with footrest and cushions, a velvet loveseat, and two large throw pillows on an oriental rug. Daphne sat in a beanbag chair and Zachary in the Adirondack chair, but he pushed the footrest aside.

Mitchell starts the session rolling with a comment that ninety-seven percent of all therapists must say. "So, tell us about yourselves and why you are here."

Zachary responds with a rough edge in his voice. "You probably know everything about us from Mildred. I do not consider you impartial mediators."

"I have never met the Pettersens," Mitchell responds. "That's why there are two of us here as therapists. I assure you, I can be an impartial advocate for you, as well as your critic, if necessary."

"Yeah, the Pettersens. They are the ones who should be in here with us. They're like blackbirds sitting on my shoulder. They are omnipresent in all Daphne's thoughts and actions."

"That's not true, and you know it, Zachary. You are always insulting my parents. That's immature and childish."

"Immature and childish? What about your comment the other night that at least you know who your parents are? What the hell was that supposed to mean?"

"Did you say that to Zachary?" Mitchell asks Daphne.

"I did, but I was angry."

"Ask her if she regrets saying it. I'm more than a little weary and tired of her flaunting these supposed noble family ties. My parents and twin brother died in a car crash when I was two years old. I was the only one who survived, and was raised by my wealthy aunt in New York. She put me through

Cornell, and I earned two doctorates. It chaps Daphne's butt that she willed me five million dollars when she died. Everything we have in this material world, we have because of her generosity and my hard work. You didn't go back for your masters until Ethan was three, so face it, our financial contributions will never be equal."

"I work just as hard as you do. Mitchell, I'm the guidance counselor in the middle school, and I'm proud of my job and what I earn."

"Did you also know that her father is principal of the high school right next door? That's how Daffy got the job in the first place."

"Don't you dare call me Daffy! You're showing your immaturity at every turn. My name is Daphne, like in Gian Lorenzo Bernini's sculpture *Apollo and Daphne*. My name goes all the way back to the Greek myth. The legend isn't Zachary and Daphne, you moron. I'm proud of my family, the Pettersen family, that's with two Ts. I'm one hundred percent Norwegian, you have no idea where you came from. You're Heinz 57. You probably have roots from everywhere including dingleberry trees. You have no ethnic identity."

"Speaking of trees, Daphne looked where she wasn't supposed to and was turned into a tree. I should be so lucky. Heinz 57, oh now that's original. Is that so? My mother's maiden name was Efner, and she's a direct descendent of President Zachary Taylor. That's who I was named after.

Oh, you have a really rare pedigree, all right. Pettersen, with two Ts, like Daffy, with two Fs. What are you supposed to be, rare Nordic stock? Just like Hansen, Olsen, Larsen, Nilsen, Johnsen, Andersen, and a thousand others just like you. Listen Ms. Gender Neutral Advocate, *sen* means *son of*. If you are so enlightened, why didn't you change the family name to Petterdatter? In your case, your name should have been Petterdotty, with four Ts, as in mentally imbalanced."

"What a crock! Just because you're named after a president, that doesn't automatically make you a leader. What did you do, Zachary Taylor Warren, look in Wikipedia? Zachary Taylor, what a laugh. One out of three people in America claims to be a descendent of Zachary Taylor. Big deal, he was President for a few months and is remembered for doing absolutely nothing. Your name is ugly. Zak, Zak, it sounds like an electronic bug catcher."

"I believe I detect some anger in this relationship," Dr. Florence Sidthern comments.

"You bet I'm angry. She and her mother spend all day planning our gender neutral family. Oh, you're of real Viking stock, all right. Your father couldn't change a flat tire in the rain and needs me to come over and sharpen his lawnmower blade."

"He has his doctorate in education, a PHD just like yours. He doesn't need to know how to repair his car. Not when he can pay a brilliant engineer like you to do it for him."

"I'm not an engineer, I'm a research scientist. Oh sure, so he can concentrate on higher subjects, like gender neutral physical education classes. Wait, let me guess, you want me to let him teach me how to be a better husband. Your mother rolls over him like he was an optional accessory. Let me know when he finds his pants."

"At least he uses what's inside his pants. Yours might as well be surrounded by moth balls, it's been inactive for so long."

"I'm sorry, we're out of time, but I feel that we've made some real progress today. I'm glad you opened a dialogue with each other. Talking is the first step to understanding. Please try to communicate with each other without any name-calling. We also ask you to sign a pledge that there be no guns, knives, mace, or death stars thrown at each other as you search for common ground. Try a gentle massage with ylang ylang oil when you are in the middle of an argument, and put on a CD of Windham Hill Ocean Sounds. See if that helps," Dr. Florence Sidthern says as she walks them out the back door.

«««‹›»»»

Returning home from a silent ride after their therapy session, Zachary and Daphne withdraw to different places in their 5,000-square-foot home on Harbor Road in Shelburne, Vermont. He goes to his study and watches the sunset over the Adirondack Mountains to the West of Lake Champlain. She watches the same sunset from her computer room, where she prepares a report for the school principal. Zachary goes outside and puts his Kevlar canoe in the water. He paddles furiously for half an hour to relieve his tensions and frustrations. He returns to the dock when it becomes too dark to paddle safely. He pulls the green canoe up onto their beach and is greeted by Emma, who is waiting on the sweeping rear deck by the sliding glass doors.

"How come you never take us with you when you go out in your canoe?"

"Hello Em. Sometimes I just want to be alone to think about stuff. We usually all go out on the sailboat."

"October is next week, and we've only been out twice all summer as a family. What good is it to live on the lake if we don't enjoy it? Are you and mom getting a divorce?"

"Absolutely not. We have disagreements, that's all. Don't worry about your Mom, she'll be fine after a head transplant."

Zachary withdraws to his study and reads a microbiological treatise about protoplasm enhancement induced by stored, implanted, electrical, micro-dry-cells. His eyes grow weary. He walks down the long hall and crawls into the right side of their king-sized bed. It is midnight and

Daphne is asleep. Actually, she sees him but is pretending to be asleep.

The next morning, a Wednesday, the four members of the Warren family wake up at 6:30. Emma has a timer on her personal TV, which is tuned to *Good Morning America*. Ethan has his TV tuned to the cable cartoon channel. This morning it's Ninja Turtles. They both turn off their TVs and go back to sleep. Daphne and Zachary have a custom-made alarm clock with pre-recorded Vermont nature sounds. It alternates between waves crashing and seagulls cawing, to a waterfall and owls hooting, to a mountain stream with bird sounds. At first the sounds are very soft, and the volume increases ever so slowly until one of them wakes up. Usually it's Zachary. He turns off the sounds and tells Daphne it's time to wake up. She grunts, turns over, and goes back to sleep. Zachary showers, shaves, gets dressed, and starts his usual morning routine.

"Em, get up. Time for breakfast. Come on." He turns on her radio, which doesn't have a remote control. He chooses the classical station that is playing Scarlatti. This annoys Emma, who is now forced up. "Go and wake up Ethan or you both will be late for school."

Zachary returns to his bedroom to wake up Daphne, but she has heard Emma's radio and is staggering around the bathroom trying to find herself in the mirror. She brushes her teeth, turns around, jumps back into bed, and pulls the comforter over her head. He returns to Emma's room, and she has turned off the radio and gone back to sleep. He is convinced that no family in America wakes up harder than the Warren family. He feels like a Marine DI.

Today he is going to do something different. He usually resorts to Plan Cym. Plan Cym is Plan Cymbal. Zachary was a drummer in a rock and roll band in college and still has his full kit set up in his study. He usually grabs a Zildjian crash cymbal and goes from bedroom to bedroom pounding on it until they all catapult out of bed, but not this morning.

He grinds some fresh Columbian coffee beans and brews a pot. He pops three Eggo waffles in the six-bay Cuisanart toaster, and reams three oranges for a fresh-squeezed glass of cold, tasty wakeup juice. It is now 7:15. They all have to be at their destinations by 8:00. Actually, he always arrives at his job at 7:45. Since he has a half-hour drive, he grabs his aluminum briefcase, starts his BMW Z8, and chuckles to himself as he pulls out of the driveway toward Essex Junction and the IBX plant.

At 8:45 he gets a frantic call from Daphne. "Why didn't you wake us up? We will all be late for school!"

"I did wake all of you up, several times. There will be a new rule in our house. Each person is responsible for waking him or herself up, and getting into the kitchen in time for breakfast. I am no longer the family alarm clock. What if I have to go out of town for a week on business? What will you do then? I know what's going on here. Our family is unhappy, and nobody wants to wake up to face the day. Did you ever think about that? Every morning at breakfast the bickering starts. From now on nothing negative will be discussed at any meals. Will you agree to this?"

"I never start the fights. You are always finding fault with either me or the kids. You're critical of everything."

"It's our job to give them guidelines, not be their buddies. You do have a point, however, and I agree not to say anything critical, even if it is constructive criticism, at any of our meals. Do you think we can accomplish this?"

"I doubt it. The arguments usually start over what we should have for dinner. It goes downhill from there. I know, we should eat out tonight because you will be too embarrassed to berate me in a public restaurant."

"I have to work until 6:30, and I know I'll be too tired to go out. I'll call for two Uncle Tony's pizzas and bring them home with me. At least we all agree on the toppings. I will also get some cannoli. Pizza seems to be the one food that puts everyone in a good mood."

"That's a good idea. For once we agree on something," Daphne says with a mournful tone of voice.

«««◇»»»

Zachary Taylor Warren has a Christine D. Morton Fellowship from Cornell University, and was one of only thirty-two Americans chosen for a Rhodes Scholarship to Oxford. He was hired by IBX, the pharmaceutical giant, three years ago. It is literally the only place in Vermont or New Hampshire where he can utilize his special talents in micro and chemical biology. There are six other scientists in the cellular branch of research and development. He is severely underemployed and is disliked by his immediate supervisor, who is jealous of his qualifications and abilities. Last month he placed a letter in Zachary's personal file accusing him of not being a team player.

Although respected by his associates, he isn't well liked because he has a quick temper, vast knowledge of the entire IBX drug formulary, and no patience to carry out instructions he knows are futile, and that will not achieve results. He likes to work independently in the state-of-the-art laboratory on the second floor of IBX's East Wing. He has developed a new muscle relaxant that has shown great promise. He combined it with an anti-depressant that IBX developed years earlier, and altered the compound formulas. This new drug was introduced to management by the R & D supervisor, who largely claimed credit for its invention. The new combination drug, as yet unnamed, dramatically lowers blood pressure while eliminating anxiety at the same time. It does all this with minimal side-effects. There still remains several years of laboratory and animal testing, but IBX is very secretive about its development. If the testing is successful, the profits could be in the hundreds of millions.

Zachary is not a political animal. He doesn't particularly care what his supervisor does. He often thinks about changing from the business world to academia. He could go to work for any university and become a tenured professor in no time. But no New England university has the lab facilities that IBX does, and he would miss the cutting edge technology. His focus is on his projects, and he is currently working on cell regeneration. The work is so advanced that his associates are hesitant to ask him for an explanation or progress reports. His supervisor, however, has ordered him to appear in a meeting with the head of R & D, and the Division Vice President. Zachary suspects that it is about the new drug, but he soon learns that there are other twists.

IBX has seven plants in the United States, one in Belgium, and one in France. The testing for the new drug is to be done jointly by the Nashville, Tennessee plant and the plant in Corbeil-Essonnes, France. Zachary was not named to the development committee, a direct slap in the face by his supervisor, who named himself to represent Research and Development. Zachary is informed that his entire department will probably be moved to the Tennessee plant. The timing is to be determined.

Zachary can read between the lines, and he knows that the cold shoulder he was given at that meeting more than hints that he will not be asked to be part of the team that moves to the other plant, not that he particularly wants to leave Vermont.

He returns to his office, one of only three in his department that has an exterior window, and closes the door. Although everyone has instructions not to put anything over the clear glass window in each door, he removes his calendar from the wall, and with a thumbtack sticks it in the wooden door over the glass window to have complete privacy. He realizes that he is now forced into the unwelcome and ugly fray of office politics. He has some decisions to make. He muses about Edward Randall's story. *Wouldn't it be insanely great to develop a new drug that changed the world?*

Zachary calls Uncle Tony's Pizza and orders dinner. He leaves work an hour early and is home at 5:30. His family is surprised to see him. They say a quick perfunctory hello and dive into the pizzas. He sarcastically says, "I'm glad to see you, too." He shrugs his shoulders and pours himself a cold beer.

Chapter Three

Zachary is obsessed with PowZak. *WD-40, brake fluid, and herbs in a clear plastic bag... Randall could have done better with the ingredients.* He's sitting at the olivewood and leather desk that belonged to his late uncle. The floor lamp is lit, and the time is 10:00 p.m. This has been his routine of late. He retreats to his study after dinner, or after one or two TV shows that the family mindlessly watches. This is to avoid interaction with Daphne. He's uncomfortable being around members of his own family, and feels guilty that he doesn't give them more of his time.

He's always been the kind of person who gets his best ideas when doing repetitive work. He can tap into that twilight zone between total relaxation and near-sleep, and conscious problem-solving. He is playing computer chess and has beaten the theoretical expert three times in a row.

Zachary has an "aha!" moment. He has been isolating molecular materials using the tools of quantum chemistry, nonequilibrium statistical mechanics, and fluid dynamics. He believes he can apply his molecular orbital calculations to organic molecules, thereby regenerating them, possibly giving them a different form. It would be like using a metal patch in a wooden body, or creating a chemical that was part plant, part mineral, and part living cell tissue. *I know I won't have access to that lab for much longer, and I've always wanted to conduct my cell regeneration experiments. They won't care what I do now, since I'm probably a lame duck. Time to get to work.*

The Rawlings Lab in the East Wing of IBX is a complex covering 55,000 square feet. There are two areas that have clean-room technology, similar to that used in computer wafer manufacturing. There are filter systems that eliminate airborne particles, so cultures do not become contaminated. All scientists and technicians who enter these areas must gown up in clean-room suits from head to foot. They must put on special fabric boots over their shoes, tied shut with draw-strings. They have special face shields with particle masks, so no human cells are accidentally shed into the environment. Zachary has been in and out of these two areas thousands of times, so the dressing and undressing has become totally routine. Any material brought into the labs has to be in sealed carriers. Special pens are used. Pencils are prohibited because even a minute amount of graphite dust can ruin months of research.

He has brought two compounds with him that he developed in the bio-chemical lab. He is one the few people authorized to use the electron microscope, which is housed in its own clean-room within the larger clean-room. IBX has one of only three highly advanced Titan 80-300 Cubed microscopes in the world. This electron microscope is so advanced that the user can easily identify atoms, measure their chemical state, and even probe the electrons that bind them together. It makes structures only nanometers high look like mountain ranges.

Zachary places both compounds, which are in small red glass beakers, on a unique warming surface that has been set to 98.6 degrees, the same temperature as a human body. He waits until the sensor tells him that the entire liquid is ready, then he removes two drops from compound A and places it in a custom crystalline indentation on the microscope stage. He controls the x and y motion axes with the computer. He observes the molecular changes, wanting to see a halo effect around each cell. His previous measurements of the cells' sizes would be compared to the same cells after being treated with the compound that he is viewing now. He quickly checks the original data and sees no changes. He raises the temperature to 150 degrees to speed up the process, but again, there are no changes in cell size. He was hoping to see a ten to fifteen percent gain in mass.

Zachary views both beakers, side by side on the warming tray, but he is puzzled. The liquid in compound B is two inches higher than in compound A. He knows he poured the exact same 29.573 ml (about one fluid ounce) into each, but now compound B has more than doubled. He quickly places a drop into another crystalline holder. Not only does he see a halo effect, but the cells have more than tripled in size. Their molecular properties have changed completely. After four minutes he takes another measurement and the cells have grown to five times their original size. When he does a spectrographic analysis of all the compounds, he finds that he has created a universal substance that combines protoplasm, minerals, metals, and electrical atoms in flux. He can change the nature of the compound by varying the frequency of the electron particles with which he bombards it. He shuts down the experiment, renders both compounds inert, and removes the data disk from the Titan's computer.

«««◇»»»

"Mom, I think that's a fabulous idea." It is Saturday morning. Daphne and Mildred are having tea and scones at the Pettersen home, and Mildred is telling her about her idea for a new elementary school. "It will be modeled after the Gargadlia School in Sweden. They take every precaution to ensure that children do not fall into gender stereotypes. They carefully choose the placement of toys and choice of books. They have a special hired 'gender pedagogue' who is a dogma watchdog. She identifies and removes language and behavior that might reinforce stereotypes."

"That's good, Ma. Society expects men to be tough, dragon-slayers, bold, and assertive. They expect women to be passive, nurturing, quiet, and pretty. That's not fair to the children."

"You bet it isn't. In Gargadlia, boys and girls play together with toy kitchen utensils placed next to construction blocks. There are no taboos over which object a child may choose. If they are playing house, the role of the person taking care of the children can be a boy, and the breadwinner of the family can be a girl."

"Hello Mildred, hello Daphne," Zachary says as he walks into the kitchen. "I bought a dozen bagels with chive cream cheese, but I see you already have scones."

"Thank you, Zachary. Would you like a scone?"

"No thanks, I'd rather have a bagel."

Mildred tells Zachary that they were discussing Gargadlia and how excited she is about the possibility of a similar school being started in Vermont. Zachary chokes on his bagel.

"Mildred, Daphne, let me give you some facts about that school. I know you're interested in gender neutral education, so I've tried to keep an open mind about it's flaws and merits. This is what I've found. At Gargadlia the books the children read are primarily concerned with homosexual couples, single parents, or adopted children. So, guess what?

The people who send their kids to Gargadlia come from homes with same-sex parents. Big surprise."

"They don't have to come from same-sex homes, Zachary," Mildred says. "Why are you so quick to criticize?"

"And why are you so quick to deny your own nature? Did you ever hear of the hormone *oxytocin*? It is present in all girls, even pre-school age. It encourages them to love and care for dolls and to play house. Boys will take the same objects and play catch with them. Girls develop verbal skills much earlier than boys. Boys develop their visual cues earlier. We are made differently, and the differences are not made to divide us, but for us to complement each other. I thought we might talk about this subject, so I brought an article written by Hannah Boyd. Here's what she says about gender differences:

"Because they are hard-wired to enjoy spatial-mechanical play, boys require more physical space than girls, and will bounce off the walls when confined. They need to run, to spread out their toys, and to sprawl.

"Boys don't hear as well as girls, and may require you to speak loudly or tap an arm to get their attention. If your son seems to ignore your instructions, ask him to repeat them back to you.

"Give him time to finish his activity before moving on to the next.

"Don't worry if you notice your son good-naturedly roughhousing with his friends; mock fighting is natural at this age and seems to be a form of early male bonding."

"And listen to this regarding girls," Zachary says.

"Even at this age, higher levels of the hormone oxytocin (which helps bond mothers to their babies) encourage girls to love and care for their dolls, while boys see them only as inanimate objects to be thrown around.

"For girls, verbal skills develop early.

"Girls tend to use all their senses, while boys rely primarily on visual cues.

"Girls of this age may flirt with their fathers; this shows not only their love for their fathers, but also their healthy identification with their mothers."

Zachary finishes with the Boyd article. "You are really trying social engineering experiments that fly in the face of biological facts. You will end up confusing children as to their normal gender role. My suggestion is to encourage children to learn about each other's roles without actually having to adopt the lifestyle. For instance, what's wrong with a boy taking a home economics or cooking class, or a girl taking a woodworking or welding class? But they should not try to change gender roles. He should be a boy who learns how to cook, or a girl who can make a chair."

"Why are you homophobic, Zachary?" Mildred asks.

"I am not homophobic, I am allergic to illogic."

"See! See! Ma, he's at it again calling us names. He just said we are illogical. It never stops. All day, all night. He did the same thing in therapy."

"So I heard."

"Heard what!" Zachary stands up in a rage. "How dare you talk to our therapist? Our relationship is none of your business! Forgive me for intruding on your little planning session, I'm out of here. I can see the graduates of your school now. Let me tell you something: homosexuals like sex, their own sex. What does a gender neutral person prefer, another gender neutral person? I'll bet the sparks really fly in those relationships. No, wait, it might work. You have a boy who thinks he's a girl, and a girl who thinks she's a boy, and they could copulate by accident. They won't know how or why it happened, but it could be a pleasant surprise. They could create a gender neutral baby from the get-go."

"You're sick!"

《《《〈〉》》》

"Zachary, don't forget. We're giving a party tonight, so please help me get things ready."

"Oh shit, I forgot about that. I really don't feel like partying, but I suppose it's too late to cancel now. Tell me how I can help. I'll even help you do girly things if you hand me a pretty apron." Zachary grabs Daphne from behind and kisses her neck. She is startled, but smiles.

"More like that, Zachary. More like that."

Three other couples arrive between 8:00 and 8:30. Two couples are neighbors and the third is from Daphne's school. Ethan and Emma are told that they can join the party but must go to their rooms at 10:00. Both Zachary and Daphne think it wise. Sometimes adults can be unpredictable at adult parties. He is going through the motions and trying to be sociable. All he can think about is his test results with the Titan microscope; perhaps the party will be a good distraction. The Warren game room is quite large. There's a chill in the air, so Zachary built a fire in the fireplace and tossed some copper-sulfate coated pine cones into the fire to create blue and green flames. It's close to midnight and everyone is happy and getting more boisterous as the drinks flow.

"I know," Daphne says. "Let's play Mad Libs." She searches in vain for the book but can't find it.

"I'll write a story if you give me a few minutes," one of their neighbors, a book publisher, says. He sits in the captain's chair by the fireplace with a yellow legal pad that Daphne gives him. He writes out a Mad Lib.

(noun), (noun), and (noun) are the three things that (female person) positively can't live without. They are almost as important as her (*noun*) and she must (verb) them to her (sex object). For three long months, every morning her (animal) and she would (verb) across town with her (sex object) and show it to all the neighbors. (exclamation)! they would shout as they threw (noun)s at her. The police arrested her for (verb) ing the (sex object) in public, and she had to spend a week in (place). When she returned home her (animal) was waiting for her holding a (noun). She was so happy that she (verb)ed across the kitchen table and (verb) ed on the living room rug. She decided to market the (sex object). She took out an ad in (publication) and decided to offer a (adjective), (adjective), and a (adjective) one. She has no doubt that they will be received well by (person) and his/her family.

"Okay, ready to play." The neighbor goes around the room and asks for words. "Okay, give me a noun, another noun, another noun, a female person." When he gets to Zachary, he asks for a sex object and Zachary answers *dildo*. The neighbor asks Daphne for a noun and she answers *saltine cracker*. When Zachary's turn comes again he is asked for an adjective and he answers *oily*.

Beetles, prunes, and carburetors are the three things that Daphne Warren positively can't live without. They are almost as important as her tulips, and she must glue them to her dildo. For three long months, every morning her chipmunk and she would glide across town with her dildo and show it to all the neighbors. Awesome! they would shout as they threw turds at her. The police arrested her for masticating the dildo in public, and she had to spend a week in Cleveland. When she returned home her chipmunk was waiting for her holding a saltine cracker. She was so happy that she pummeled across the kitchen table and oscillated on the living room rug. She decided to market the dildo. She took out an ad in AARP Magazine and decided to offer a corpuscular, an oily, and a gritty one. I have no doubt that they will be received well by Kim Kardashian and her family.

《《《〈〉》》》

Sunday morning breakfast was later than usual. Zachary was up first and made everyone pecan waffles. Daphne drank way too much, left the party early, and went to bed. She was upset that she was the center of attention. This had never happed to her before in a group setting in front of her neighbors and peers, and she felt uneasy in retrospect.

"Mom, what's a dildo?" Ethan asks as he pours fancy grade maple syrup on his waffles.

Zachary laughs, but Daphne says "See, see, they don't miss anything. You don't think they can hear us at the other end of the house, but you're wrong. It's nothing you need be concerned about, Ethan."

"It's a fake penis," Zachary answers.

"Why would anyone need a fake penis when they can have a real one?" Ethan asks.

"Who would want a real one?" Emma counters. "I can live perfectly well without one."

"You wish you had one," Ethan taunts Emma.

"Do not!"

"Yes, you do. Some day I'm going to be tougher than you and I'm going to beat you up."

"In your dreams, little man."

"Okay, that's enough. Be quiet and eat your breakfast, or get up from the table and go to your rooms," Zachary barks.

Daphne's cellphone rings. "Quiet, I can't hear." She walks away from the kitchen table. "Oh hello, Mr. Bertram, no that's fine, this isn't a bad time for me to talk." She walks out of the kitchen and into the dining room. She talks to Mr. Bertram, the principal of her middle school, for fifteen minutes and returns ashen-faced to the kitchen.

"That's about me, isn't it?" Emma says.

"Why didn't you tell us? Why do I have to hear it from the principal?"

"What's going on?" Zachary asks.

"Em is in big trouble. Ethan, please go to your room. We want to talk to Em."

"Ha ha, Em's a dildo, she's in trouble, ha ha."

"That's enough, Ethan, go to your room. Now!" Zachary shows his anger. "Daphne, don't tell me what's going on, I want to hear it from Em." He makes a beckoning gesture with his right hand toward his daughter.

"It's really no big deal. A lot of kids are doing it."

"Doing what, Emma Warren? Are you going to tell me or aren't you?" Zachary is running out of patience. Emma sits at the kitchen table with her arms folded but doesn't say anything.

Daphne answers for her. "They did a routine inspection and found a bag of marijuana in her locker. Since I'm the guidance counselor of her school, there's a conflict, so she has to see someone else. You're very lucky, young lady, that I have the position that I do, because without me, we would all be hauled into family court. Is that what you want?"

"I don't know why they make such a big deal out of it. Lot's of kids smoke grass. Some do crack and meth. You smoked when you were younger, so don't be hypocrites. At least they didn't find condoms like they did in Carol's locker."

"This is what I'm going to do." Zachary is speaking calmly but is in an internal rage. "The first thing I'm going to do is go back with you to your room. I'm going to ask you to show me where you have drugs hidden. If you don't show me, I'm going to tear your entire room apart, everything you own. If I find any, you will be left with a bed and a chair. No TV, no little refrigerator, no texting. You will then be grounded for a year. You will come home right after school, and if you so much as squeak, you're going to wish you belonged to another family. Is that clear?"

Zachary is six foot three inches tall. When he's angry, his face turns red and his muscles bulge like the Incredible Hulk. On one occasion when he lost his temper at Cornell, he punched through a two-inch-thick, straight-back oak chair. It was an antique that belonged to his fraternity house. Daphne can see that he is about to lose control.

"Zachary, please let me handle this. I know you have Em's best interests at heart, but let me handle this. Okay?"

"We should both handle this."

"I agree, but let me handle it first. Okay?"

Zachary throws his arms out in a gesture of futility and walks out of the kitchen. He decides to go to IBX and work on compound B.

Chapter Four

"And good evening to the Warren family," Dr. Florence Sidthern says as she walks into the waiting room. As usual, the couple sits there in silence, each reading the same magazine they were reading before their first session. Mitchell is in his familiar place, holding a clipboard and a blue-striped celluloid Pelikan fountain pen.

"How are things with you guys,?" Mitchell asks.

"Fine, everything in our family is just fine, absolutely peachy, right as rain, not a cloud in sight," Zachary replies.

"That's not true," Daphne says. "Our daughter Emma is in trouble."

"Then why did you say that everything is fine, Zachary?" Mitchell inquires.

"I know nothing about this. I was told by Daphne that she is to handle Em's problem, and she has told me nothing. That was Sunday morning, and it is now Tuesday evening. We were informed that our daughter had marijuana in her locker. She's been sent for counseling at another school since her brilliant mother is the counselor at Em's middle school. So if you want information about our family, please don't talk to me."

"I had to back you off. You don't know how threatening you can look to a thirteen-year-old girl. Making her cower in fear is not the answer. We need to reach out to her and let her know that what she's doing is wrong, but without shouting. When you lose your temper, you lose your power. She needs steady, firm discipline, not a momentary tantrum."

"Let me tell you what Emma has done in the last six months. First she makes her mother buy her a weight bench. Then she petitions to join the boys' soccer team because she is faster and tougher than they are. Two months ago she got into a fight with a boy—this is not a girl, this is a boy—and his parents are suing us because he now needs two new teeth and a bridge. One month ago I heard a loud bang and went into our basement. There was Emma with my .38 caliber revolver, shooting into a stack of newspapers. She didn't have on hearing protection. I grabbed the gun and asked her what she was doing, and she said she was trying to see if hollow point bullets did a lot of damage like she saw on television."

"I told you not to leave your gun lying around!"

"It wasn't lying around. It has a special lock on the hammer, the ammo is stored in a different place in my top closet, and the key to the gun is kept on my key ring, which is in a basket with my wallet in a table drawer in our hall. She had to go through quite a sequence to load and activate the weapon. But I don't really see the problem. In your gender neutral world, she is doing what any healthy red-blooded boy would do: get into fights, use guns, use drugs."

"So you're blaming me for Em's problems? That's not fair. You always include Ethan in your boy pursuits and Em feels left out. She's overreacting because she doesn't have enough attention from her father."

"Good Doctors, I feel that there is more than an element of truth in what she is saying. Yes, I don't spend enough time with her, but Daphne gives the kids mixed messages about gender expectations. Let's face it, neither of us knows what we're doing, and we should never have been parents. You have to learn how to be an adult before you can parent a child."

"Oh, that's a big help, Zachary. What do you expect us to do, return them to WalMart? We're their parents, so we had better get it right."

"Look Daphne-with-one-D, you let Ethan play with dollies to make sure he's thweet, and you are trying to turn our daughter into Emma the Emasculator. Do you hate men that much? I've tried to soften the girl and teach her kindness, but there is only so much I can do."

"It's Emma's life," Daphne counters. "She doesn't want to be a weak sister in a rough world. As a man, you should understand that."

"I understand nothing. We do not agree on one item about raising our children."

"So where does that leave us?" Daphne snaps. "Do you want to divorce me? If you do, I will demand custody."

"If we divorce, we will obviously have to share custody. In other words we will continue the same bullshit as we pass them back and forth. We have got to stop living our own sorry lives through our children, and start thinking about them and their welfare."

"I don't have a sorry life! I don't know what that means!" Daphne says, reaching for a tissue in her purse.

Florence says, "It means you have to come back next week because we're out of time."

Zachary says, "Sure, sure, at least it gives you therapists a steady income. At this rate of non-progress, we'll be grandparents before we're decent parents."

"Why don't you try being parents to each other? Daphne can be your mommy, Zachary, and Zachary can be your daddy, Daphne. If you learn how to parent each other, you can then make your children your grandparents." Florence says as she studies her new manicure. "If you switch roles, you can learn how the other person feels. You'll all be so confused, you won't have time for any psychopathology."

《《《〈〉》》》

Zachary's breakthrough discovery of cell regeneration is now consuming all his energy. He is even more distant than usual at home, and at IBX he works in total isolation. In honor of Edward Randall's story, he names compound B PowZak. He's not sure what the limits of his new drug are, and more to the point, he doesn't as yet fully understand its basic properties. He decontaminates the movable scanning equipment and wheels it into the clean-room next to the Titan microscope. He is studying the effects of different radiation on the size and growth rate of the cells. He focuses normal electron beams, low-energy secondary electron beams, and high-energy backscattered beams. He uses X-ray emissions and studies the ultraviolet wavelengths in the aura around the cells.

He is able to control the growth rate by regulating the amplitude and frequency of the electrons. He has crossed the line into uncharted territory by merging organic and inorganic chemistry. He wants to shout his discovery to the world, but decides to do just the opposite. Zachary needs to do more research, but he is so close to creating a wonder drug, a drug that may be able to clone life itself.

It is Friday afternoon at 1:00. Zachary ate his lunch in his office. The day before, he finalized his research on PowZak. He has a theory that can only be tested by putting the researcher at great risk. No animals can be used because the subject must have a consciousness of life. He is convinced there can be a direct connection between the path and intensity of human brain waves, and the effect these brain waves have on the PowZak cells. This is much the same as the electrical stimulation done with the Titan microscope. The human brain energy will direct and change the cells if they are ingested by a researcher, by him. The PowZak cells will then combine with all his other cells. His theory is that by unthinking the change, he could then return his system to his prior state as willed by his brain.

But what if he can't return back to his original form? What if he wills that he be three inches taller, and the drug makes it so. Perhaps, even though he wants to return to his original height, the changes may be permanent. This is a risk he is not willing to take. He must think of a test on a much smaller scale, one that doesn't involve so much risk.

Since Zachary is convinced that he will soon be leaving IBX, he prepares a liter of his PowZak and destroys all evidence of its creation. He replaces the hard drives in the microscope and the electronic scanners. He also replaces the hard drive on his office computer. There will be no trace of his discovery.

His timing is perfect, because late Friday afternoon Zachary is called into the vice president's office and told that he must gather his personal possessions and leave the building. He is thanked for his contributions but told that the entire department is being restructured, blah, blah, blah.

»«««◊»»»«

"Hello everyone," Zachary says as he walks in the door with two Uncle Tony's pizzas, and a covered plastic tray full of cannoli.

"You're home early," Daphne says. "I'm not particularly glad to see you, but I am glad to see the pizzas," she adds with a big grin. Emma and Ethan both shout, "Pizza!"

Zachary isn't used to hearing humor from his wife and is surprised.

"I'm kidding, Zachary. I'm almost as glad to see you as I am the cannoli."

He places the boxes on the kitchen table and hugs Daphne. She senses that something is wrong, but doesn't ask him.

"I'm going to get out of these work clothes. I'll be right back. If you two eat all the pizza, you will die."

Daphne follows him into their bedroom. "I lost my job today. They say it was due to restructuring, but the R & D boss is a....."

"He's a shithead," Daphne interrupts. "I always knew he had it in for you, ever since I met him at the Christmas party. He is sooo jealous. What are you going to do now?"

"Thanks for being so kind. I really mean it. Yes, he is a dildo, to use the new family word. I don't know. I guess I can do anything I want. Start my own company, go to work for a college, write books, take a few years off, become a shape-shifter."

"Become a what?"

"Nothing. Let's eat some pizza."

Zachary feels as if he is in the center of a spoked wheel. Each spoke is a different path leading out from the present. He now finds himself, at age thirty-six, in a full-fledged midlife crisis. *Isn't this a bit early?* he quips to himself as he takes a bite out of a delicious pizza slice with garlic, meatballs, and peppers. *I have no job, Daphne and I don't have sex, our children are a mess, and I've discovered something that I dare not share with the world and am afraid to test.*

"Hey kids, do you know what I'm going to do? I left my job. As you know, jobs come and go. I'm going to start my own consulting company and work from the house. That means we can do more things together. Em, I'll be able to drive you back and forth to soccer practice. That will give your mother a break. Who wants to go for a sailboat cruise to Willsboro Bay tomorrow?"

"I have soccer practice at eleven," Emma responds.

"Nathan and Tom are coming over tomorrow, Dad. We're going to play video games."

"It's a bit late in the season," Daphne says. "It's supposed to be chilly and rainy tomorrow. Perhaps next weekend."

It's a bit late in the season. Daphne's words echo like a brick thrown down a well. Zachary withdraws to his study. He places his PowZak compound, his notebook computer, and some electronic testing equipment in his closet. He had a huge lock placed on it, after the gun incident with Emma. He now stores the .38 in the closet. He is the only one who knows the combination.

He turns on his desktop computer and does research on shape-shifters. He used the word when talking to Daphne and wonders if there is such a thing, or if it is a creation of the *Deep Space 9* television series. He finds that the idea originated way back in human history, to the ancient Greeks and even earlier. The idea is present in everything from mythology to folklore, epic poems, Shakespearean comedy, even ballet. This is in addition to all the modern usage in film, television, and video games.

According to legend, a shape-shifter is capable of changing its shape into that of another person, creature, or even an object. The change can be induced voluntarily by the use of a magic potion, by an act of will, or involuntarily by a curse or a deity's malevolence. The changes may or may not be permanent. There are many incidents in literature of both. He reads a paragraph from an article in Wikipedia. "In her *Earthsea* books, Ursula K. Le Guin depicts an animal form as slowly transforming the wizard's mind, so that the dolphin, or bear, or other creature forgets it was human and cannot change back, a voluntary shape-shifting becoming an imprisoning metamorphosis."

An imprisoning metamorphosis—this is what Zachary feared if his PowZak changes cannot be reversed. There are many examples in literature. Italo Calvino's *The Canary Prince* is a story where a shape-shifter gains access to a tower to free the princess. Gender shifting has been used as a disguise. Zeus disguised himself as Artemis to get close enough to Callisto that she couldn't escape.

Whoa, this really gets interesting. He continues to read from the Wikipedia site. "In Greek mythology, the young Tiresias was walking through a forest when he found two snakes in the act of love. He prodded them with a stick and was instantly changed into a woman. He lived in this female form for many years, and even married and had children. Years later, Tiresias came across the same snakes doing the same thing. Again she poked them with a stick, and Tiresias turned back into a man. Later in his life, he was asked by Zeus which of the two genders enjoys sex more. Tiresias, speaking from experience, replied that it is the woman, and Hera blinded him for telling her husband of the greatest secret of women. Zeus, unable to undo what his wife had done, gave the now blind Tiresias the gift of foresight."

Zachary wonders how it would be if he were a woman. He reads about the legend of Apollo and Daphne. He made fun of his wife's comments, but this is another example of shape-shifting. An unwilling Daphne turned into a tree. Zachary hasn't lost interest in sex; it's just that he, well, he knows it isn't about Daphne, because she is still gorgeous. It's about himself. He often finds fault with others because he can't face himself.

He remembers another fairy tale. In *The Frog Prince*, a prince is turned into a frog because he was vain and conceited. Only a kiss from a beautiful princess could return him back into his human form. Zachary wonders if he is the frog.

Wow, when I think of it, there are many examples of shape-shifters. Look at Pygmalion, who fell in love with Galatea, the statue he had carved. Aphrodite had pity on him and transformed the marble into a living woman. Then there are werewolves who morph from humans into ugly, hairy wolves. Vampires change into bats, or can appear from a puff of smoke. Dr. Jekyll changed into Mr. Hyde by drinking a potion. Some of the legends say that a prop of some kind is needed. The changeling needs an article of clothing or another possession before a transformation can occur. Dorian Gray had his portrait in the closet change instead of himself. That was a creative twist.

His favorite story of all is *Metamorphosis*, by Franz Kafka. Poor Gregor Samsa woke up one morning to find that he couldn't turn over in bed because he changed into a cockroach. How can a man-sized insect possibly exist in the world? What a wonderful story. Kafka made it believable. He gave Gregor a pathetic end. He was unable to return to work, and his father injured him with a stick, forcing him back through the door and into his room. Gregor hides under the couch, where he feels more comfortable. The only fun he has is climbing the walls and ceiling. For years his family hadn't told him about the money saved from his father's collapsed business, and Gregor had supported everyone. In the end, his family shunts him aside. His sister hates being in his presence, and he has to cover himself with a sheet. When he escapes from his room, his father throws apples at him and injures Gregor further.

In the end, his sister Grete tells their parents they have to get rid of Gregor. They tell him that if he really loved his family, he would have left home and spared them. Gregor knows his sister is right and that he should disappear. He returns to his room, and dies at sunrise.

Zachary wonders what his family would do if he were suddenly turned into a giant cockroach. *First of all, they would all scream in terror. Emma would reach for the Hot Shot, Daphne would call the police, and Ethan would think it was a neat new video game.* He laughs at the thought of going into a therapy session and sprawling across two large cushions on the Oriental rug. *Would Florence tell me I was having an identity crisis?* "You're really beginning to bug me," *Mitchell would say.* "You're not sleeping in my bed with a body like that," *Daphne would comment.* "I never saw anyone with so many legs. How are you going to find running shoes?" "Do you have a penis?" *Poor Gregor.*

Zachary tries to feel sorry for himself, but fails miserably. He counts his assets: his sprawling house on the lake, sailboat, BMW Z8, solid financial security, great health, family, accomplishments, and realizes he is the sole source of his discontent. Sometimes the only thing to do is nothing. He shuts down his computer and sits in his favorite chair. Instead of reading a scientific journal, he chooses another story by Edward Randall. He gets only five pages into it before falling soundly asleep with the light on.

Chapter Five

"Daphne, I can tell that Emma is way less than thrilled to have me around the house. Perhaps I cramp her style. I demand to know what's going on with her drug situation."

"The first thing I'm trying to do is win her trust. She's traveling back and forth with me to school, except when she has soccer practice or a meeting with the drama club."

"How often is that, twice a week?"

"Three or four times a week."

"In other words, you really have no idea whether or not she is still using pot. Does she still hang out with those girls who had condoms taken from their lockers?"

"No, I don't know if she's still using pot, and I don't know if she is still friendly with those girls."

"They're thirteen and fourteen years old, for Christ's sake. If we don't do something, Daphne, she will be lost. We can't permit that."

"What would you suggest? Do we prevent her from going to school? Do we pull her out of that school, where I can see some of what she's doing, and put her in a private school, where she will do much worse? The changes have to come from within."

"Daphne, I don't think we can wait for that to happen. She doesn't respect me, and I demand respect."

"You can't demand respect. You can demand obedience, you can demand compliance, but you can't demand respect. Respect has to be earned. There is no quick fix here. It's going to be a long, hard road, and you have to be ready for a one-hundred-percent time commitment. *Are* you ready for that?"

Zachary knows that Daphne has spoken the truth. He nods his head in the affirmative and reassures her that he will not get heavy. "We'll try it your way. I don't know what else we can do."

The temperature is fifty-three degrees. It's sunny and there is no wind. The leaves have mostly fallen from the trees, but there are some solid yellow patches of color on late-changing sugar maples. He takes out his canoe and paddles close to the shore. He glides around the Shelburne Marina and into the bay. He paddles into a fresh breeze from the south, and he finds it's great exercise to make any headway. He reaches the rocky cliff by the state access area at the end of Shelburne Bay and turns the canoe around to head home. Halfway up the bay the wind shifts to the north, and he is again paddling into the wind as he heads home.

The activity frees his thoughts. The family has enough money to live on for a while. He will not start a consulting company, but he will use the idea as a cover for other operations. He will concentrate on understanding and developing PowZak. He may have to access research facilities in other states, perhaps at M.I.T. or Cornell. He can maintain the ruse that he is networking for his new business.

Zachary is not the kind of man who can sit and do nothing. He is never satisfied to let something take its course, or wait until an understanding is reached. He always forces a solution to aggressively solve a problem. He decides that without risk, there are no rewards.

He decides to use himself for the first test of PowZak.

《《《《〇》》》》

Zachary tells his family that he will be working in isolation and doesn't want to be disturbed unless there is an emergency. Daphne protests. "I presume I'm still good enough to cook your meals. Will there be anything else, Massa?" He calmly tells her that it is his responsibility to do whatever is necessary support the family, even if it means his commuting to another city.

Zachary has the door to his study closed, and it is locked from the inside. He has the blinds drawn on the windows facing the lake. *Emma is still doing drugs; I know it.* He's piecing together behavior patterns that have changed in her routines. She is now meticulous about washing her clothes daily. She used to throw them in the hamper to be done with all the other clothes on laundry day. He theorizes that the reason is the smell of the marijuana. She doesn't want her parents to detect any odor. She also showers twice a day now instead of only in the morning, so we won't smell the drugs on her hair.

There are hundreds of hiding places in her room where she could stash the pot. He would literally have to tear everything apart. This would start a war, alienate Daphne, and frighten Ethan. What if he could enhance his sense of smell? He could use a small amount of PowZak and give himself a mild electric stimulation, just a couple of milliwatts. He wants to amplify his reception to the wave-like properties of odor molecules. These molecules will cause the PowZak-heightened electrons in his nasal receptors to send strong signals to his brain. Different odors have different frequencies. He will be able to analyze the various electrical vibrations and isolate odors that are not even detectable by humans.

Zachary knows, since there have been no tests, that he is flying blind as to the amount of PowZak he should take. He doesn't want to overdo the amount, but he has to start somewhere. Perhaps a few drops are all that will be needed.

He knows the secret of his success will be mental discipline. The drug, its path, its effectiveness or lack thereof, will all be controlled by his thoughts. He has been practicing meditation. In the Buddhist sense, he has a Monkey Mind. He finds it difficult to focus on one subject to the exclusion of everything else. In many ways he is like a giant SETI parabolic radio antenna that is listening for alien broadcasts. Disregarding superfluous information will be vital if he is to control the process. If he lets his thoughts wander, or if he becomes distracted, the results could be very different from what he intends.

He pours a double of his favorite Chivas Regal twenty-five-year-old Scotch. He places a small amount of PowZak into a red beaker and grabs an eyedropper with a special non-absorbent polymer bulb. The beaker is in his left hand, and the eyedropper is in his right. Both hands are shaking. He puts the eyedropper in the beaker and squeezes the bulb until the dropper is half full. He controls the shaking in his hands by remaining motionless for several minutes. When he is calm, he places two drops into the Scotch. He squeezes the rest back into the containment vessel and uses the pump to remove all air. The eyedropper will be flushed thoroughly with the special antidote that will render PowZak inert.

The antidote is a molecular cancelling agent that has opposing formulas, and is completely stable in a normal environment. Oddly enough, it's a slight adaptation of his original compound A. By mixing the exact same amount of A with PowZak, the effects will be cancelled even if the host's thoughts are bent on continuation. He can also cancel the effects himself by his will and return to normal. He must never let even a minute amount of PowZak be flushed down a drain, or disposed of in any form without being treated with compound A.

Zachary has prepared a message. In the event of his death, he wants the formula and all the technical information to be given to Cornell University. He has all the data on both his notebook and desktop hard drives. He decided against any personal notes to his family or to his former associates at the University. He chose to keep the communication brief and strictly related to the safekeeping and use of PowZak.

His thoughts are racing fast-frame. *What if this is a total bust, and doesn't work? What if it just kills me cold? At least I have a great insurance policy.* He remembers July 1969, the first man on the moon. *Neil Armstrong said, "That's one small step for a man, one giant leap for mankind." Alexander Fleming discovered penicillin. Jonas Salk cured polio. Louis Pasteur made milk safe to drink. What will PowZak do?*

Zachary lifts the shade and looks at the sun about to sink below the Adirondack Mountains. It's sending a single red finger across the water, illuminating the white hull of their sailboat tied to the dock. He thinks of the timelessness of nature, the reassuring existence of Earth, but is unsure of his place in the cosmos, or even in his own family. He raises the glass, salutes the sun as it dips below the mountains, and drinks the Scotch in two quick gulps.

Emma is in a jovial mood and is in Ethan's room playing the Guitar Hero video game. Zachary takes this opportunity to enter her room, and with his heightened awareness, he searches for drugs. His senses tell him that there is marijuana hidden inside one of her computer speakers. She must have taken the back off and stuck it inside. When he examines the Phillips-head screws, he sees shiny places where the black paint has worn. There are only four screws, and it would be easy for her to take the back off. He hears Emma walking down the hall and quickly leaves her room.

"Whoa, who let you in here?" Emma says excitedly. "Mom, Dad, there's a big dog in the house." Emma tries to grab the dog, but he scoots by her down the hall, reaches up with his front paw, opens the sliding glass door handle, and runs toward the back of the garage. Emma is in hot pursuit, but the dog runs out of sight and she meets Zachary who comes around from the front of the garage.

"Dad, did you see that dog? How did he get in?"

"Yes I did, he...uh...ran down the block. He must belong to a neighbor. I don't know how he got in. Perhaps through our doggy door."

"Aw, really Dad, we don't have a doggy door."

"Perhaps he has a passkey. I don't know, Em, what kind of dog was he?"

"It was a police dog, and he smelled funny. Like he had been drinking."

"Are you sure it wasn't a Saint Bernard, Em? They usually carry flasks of brandy. He sounds harmless enough. Come on, let's go inside."

Zachary calmly walks into the bathroom. He puts one hand over each ear, cries and laughs at the same time, and throws up into the toilet.

《《《《〈〉》》》》

Why? He has been pacing in his study trying to analyze what happened. After the dog incident yesterday, he sat down with the family for the evening meal. Daphne made quiche Lorraine, but all he wanted was to gnaw on a T-bone steak. While he was sitting at the dining room table, he was overcome with fear. What if he can't purge his mind and suddenly morphs into a dog right in front of his family? He excused himself and went back into his study. Zachary concentrated on his sense of smell and stared at his reflection on the blank computer screen. Sure enough, he changed back into a dog. He was now a huge white Saint Bernard with brown patches and a bottle of Courvoisier cognac hung around his neck. *I though Emma said I was a police dog. But that was when I was sniffing for drugs. When I last spoke of a dog I mentioned the Saint Bernard.*

Obviously that was still on my subconscious mind. When I think of brandy, I think of Courvoisier.

He took two drops of compound A antidote and waited a few minutes for it to work. He again concentrated on his canine persona but he observed no change in his reflection. The craving for a T-bone disappeared. Confident now that he would remain himself, he rejoined his family. He confirms to himself that all changes are the result of his thoughts. He wonders what the limits of PowZak will be.

Today, Sunday, is his family's favorite day. It's usually quiet time, with each member engaged in private pursuits, but yet they interact at meals, and sometimes play a game. They always watch a movie. Lately, Zachary and Daphne fight about whether or not a film is suitable for children. Emma and Ethan are always there for the PG-13 rated movies, and lately a few R-rated films got by their parents' censorship.

Emma and Ethan are each in their room. Emma is listening to music, and Zachary is very upset because he knows the drugs are inside her stereo speaker.

"Daphne, will you come with me into Em's room? There's something we have to do. I know where she hides her pot. I promised you I would not get heavy, and I'm not going to. All I need is your support. I have an idea that may work."

"What are you going to do? You have to tell me."

"I'm not exactly sure, but I'm going to count on oxytocin."

"No, Zachary, please, not without more thought."

"Daphne, I'm going in there with or without you. It's your choice."

Emma is reading Macbeth for a language arts assignment when her parents enter the room. Zachary asks her to turn the music off.

"Em, I'm amazed that you can read something as demanding as Macbeth and still be able to listen to music. You are obviously brilliant, and take after me."

"Ha ha," Daphne says nervously, but is reassured by Zachary's manner.

He takes out a Phillips screwdriver and removes the speaker back. Daphne closes Emma's bedroom door and he takes a bag of pot from inside the speaker.

"Looks like you found my shit. I'm impressed; how did you do it? You have obviously been snooping in my room."

"I could see the paint scraped off the screws, and when I shook the speaker I could hear that something was inside."

"This doesn't change anything. What are you going to do, forbid me to go to school? Are you going to make me quit the drama club or the soccer team? Are you going to take away my television? I don't really care."

"Em, we're not going to do any of those things," Zachary says, handing the half-ounce bag of drugs to his daughter. "Don't you feel that everyone should smoke pot, and lie to their parents? If it's good for you, shouldn't be good for everyone? Wait a minute Em, I'm going to call Ethan in here and I want you to share the marijuana with him."

Zachary opens the door to Emma's room and raises his voice. "Hey Ethan, little buddy, please come to Em's room. She has something she wants to share with you."

Ethan quickly responds, but Emma runs past him into the bathroom and slams the door. She flushes the pot down the toilet. Zachary leaves the screwdriver behind and asks Daphne not to talk to Em just yet.

Zachary stands outside the bathroom door and hears Emma crying. "Em, we're going to make ravioli using the new Atlas pasta maker I bought. This is your last chance to help decide what the filling will be, if you care to join us."

"Daphne, let her come to us."

«««◊»»»

Zachary turns to page twenty-three of the cookbook that came with the pasta maker. The semolina dough has been kneaded. He loves to slam it down on the sturdy butcher-block table. He knows from his bread-baking that the dough should be slightly tacky to the touch. The instructions say to cover it in plastic and let it sit for thirty minutes. Daphne made two types of filling. She has a bowl with the traditional ricotta and spinach, and another with a savory pumpkin filling, because that is one of Emma's favorite flavors. Emma is in her bedroom and has not joined the family.

While the dough sits, Zachary reads from the instructions. "You cut a small portion about three inches wide, five inches long, and one inch thick, and feed it through the Atlas with the dial set to number one. You do this three times. Then you move the dial to number three and run it through three more times. Finally, you move the dial to number six, the thinnest setting." He is sitting on a stool in front of the pasta maker when Emma walks into the kitchen.

"I'm about to crank the dough through the machine. Do you want to have a go at it?" Emma sits on her father's lap, throws her arms around him and cries.

"What's wrong with Em? Has she been a dildo again?" Ethan says as Zachary carries Emma back to her room, followed by Daphne. Ten minutes later the three of them appear, and the Warren family all take turns cranking the Atlas machine. They make way too much ravioli and have to freeze three aluminum pans full. After dinner Daphne disappears into the bedroom.

Zachary leaves his study and locks the door from the outside. When Zachary enters the bedroom, Daphne locks the door from the inside. She informs her husband that he will not be considered for the board of trustees in the new gender neutral school that her mother is planning. She says this while she is completely naked except for white satin thong panties that Zachary promptly takes off.

"That doesn't sound like their usual fighting," Ethan says.

"It isn't," Emma responds, as the two of them listen outside their parents' bedroom door.

"Does this have anything to do with a gertoodle or a dildo?" Ethan asks Emma.

Chapter Six

Daphne and Zachary are sitting in the Sidtherns' waiting room.

"I know she will be all right now." Daphne is excited. "I can't believe the change in the last two days. Today she sat in the front seat of the car next to me and made me turn off the radio because she wanted to talk. For the entire trip she talked nonstop about how much fun it was to make ravioli. I didn't mention one word about the drugs. Ethan was jealous and called her a dildo again when we let him out in front of his school. After we dropped him off, she asked me if she was the one who brought us back together. I couldn't help it; I burst into tears right then and there and had to pull off the road. I hugged her so hard. How did you know what Em would do?"

"I didn't. I don't really know much about anything."

Dr. Florence Sidthern welcomes them and walks with the Warrens into the therapy room. Mitchell is sitting in his usual chair, holding his usual clipboard and usual fountain pen. Daphne sits in the Adirondack chair, and Zachary sits in a beanbag chair that he tosses next to Daphne's chair. It lands with a solid thud on the floor, which startles Florence. "It seems that you have decided to sit in different places this evening and very close together."

Mitchell writes on his clipboard.

Florence claps her hands together. "Today we're going to talk about sex. I don't want either of you to be embarrassed. I assure you we've heard it all."

"Did you ever hear of a transgendered menage a trois having sex together with their sheep, goats, and a horny porcupine in the same king-sized bed?" Zachary asks in total seriousness.

"No." Florence giggles.

"Then you haven't heard everything. How do you know that what we're about to tell you won't shock you? Are you prepared to control the terrible demons you are about to unleash?" Zachary continues talking with a deadpan expression.

Daphne laughs so hard she has to leave the room and go to the bathroom. She returns three minutes later, seemingly in control, but acts like a child who anticipates being tickled. She is again ready to explode, and has to stifle her laughter.

Mitchell writes on his clipboard.

"I'm assuming that you have had sex with each other at some point," Mitchell says with a hint of sarcasm in his voice. He has been unresponsive to Zachary's humor.

"Not really," Zachary responds. "Our children may look like us, but they are the byproducts of Daphne's sister and my brother who are also married and look exactly like us. We're just renting them for a year or two. Just because we have children, it isn't totally logical and safe to assume that we have had sex, or that I know what to do with my penis."

"How often do the two of you make love?" Florence asks. "Frequency is important because..."

"No, it isn't," Mitchell interrupts with annoyance. "Frequency is only a part of the whole picture. The quality of their lovemaking is equally important."

"Mitchell, it's a combination of quality and quantity. I know that. But one quality screw a year doesn't quite work for me, and probably not for them. I was merely trying to determine what the quantity is, since that is one of the two criteria we have to consider," Florence says with a nasty edge to her voice. "Daphne, how many times have you and Zachary made love in the last three months?"

"Three times: twice last night and once the night before."

Zachary asks the therapists how many times they have made love in the last three months. "Perhaps we can learn by your example."

"This isn't about us. It's about the two of you."

"That's right, Mitchell, it's not about us. We're too busy fixing other people's marriages to worry about our own," Florence says as she folds her arms in a protective posture.

"This isn't the appropriate time to discuss our problems," Mitchell says with annoyance. "For God's sake, Florence, show some professionalism."

"Tell me something, Florence and Mitchell. When you go to an auto mechanic, which one would you choose? Would you choose the guy who drives a broken-down old jalopy that is misfiring on two cylinders, or would you choose the mechanic whose car rides fast and smooth?" Zachary asks.

Mitchell writes on his clipboard.

Florence reaches into the drawer on the right side of the desk where Mitchell is sitting and shows a small box to Daphne. "This is a DVD made by Norma and William Merchant. They're sex therapists, like we are, and they live and practice in San Diego. This is a wonderful tape that shows how you can rekindle a relationship. First you speak nicely to each other. Next, you simultaneously eat a large-sized Snickers candy bar, one from each end. While listening to a Yanni CD, you then massage each other with ylang ylang oil. On the DVD they show you the right places to touch each other to induce pleasure in your partner. Do you have a wide-screen TV in your bedroom that you can see from the bed? Believe me, this is a good investment, and it's only $79.95 plus Vermont sales tax."

"Thank you, but I don't think we need the tape," Zachary says. We're both using our tongues, and we screw like rabbits until we're totally exhausted. Then we rest and do it again."

Mitchell writes on his clipboard.

"See, I told you! Oral sex is not just for college kids," Florence says as she walks the Warrens out the back door. "We'll see you next Tuesday night, if Mitchell and I are still together."

《《《《◇》》》》

Zachary is alone in the house. Daphne and the kids are at school, and he paces like a caged leopard back and forth in the hall outside his study. He realizes that, as a couple, the two of them are basically healthier than the therapists who are treating them. His daughter is quickly changing from a terrible problem to a total joy. He no longer has to contend with a stressful and demeaning job. His initial experimentation with PowZak was done from a place of internal desperation and depression. Now he's not so anxious to ruin his life. He questions his maturity.

The weather is getting cold. The temperature today will be only in the high forties. He takes the canoe out anyway, staying close to shore. He knows the "rule of fifty" that gives a person a fifty-fifty chance of living fifty minutes in water that's fifty degrees. Staying close to shore with his life-jacket on, he's stacking the deck in his favor. Paddling always makes him think. He sees an osprey nest, but the occupant is out. He also spots a great horned owl sleeping in a large oak that was about a hundred feet from the water's edge. The bird was huge. The timelessness of nature is a theme that has resonated with Zachary his whole life.

There are things that are bigger than he is. The preservation of Earth is more important than he is, or than his family is. PowZak is bigger than he is. In Edward Randall's story, it ruined Ralph's life. In the end, he was sitting in a broken-down car, in another man's body, watching as his wife left him. It frightens Zachary that there's the possibility that unlocking the drug's secrets will hurt the wonderful relationship he has rekindled with his family, yet he refuses to believe that this is a choice he must make.

He is a scientist. He will accept the challenge to further test his drug without harming himself or those he loves. A soldier called into battle does his duty. The pursuit of empirical physical evidence in the understanding and development of PowZak is no less a calling. He thought of handing his discovery and all his research to Cornell, but he's afraid that the military might get involved. He doesn't want his new drug to do harm to anyone. *So far my track record is fine. I found Em's pot, and it brought Daphne and me back together. As she said, "More like that."*

Since he's been married to Daphne, Zachary has learned the beauty and the burden of introspection. Her whole family analyzes everything they do from every possible minute angle. He remembers the Albert Camus quote: *An intellectual is someone whose mind watches itself.* He laughs and thinks, *The Sidtherns are plumbers with leaky faucets.*

As soon as a developing person has an awareness of self, he or she will hone his or her greatest talents. As a four-year-old child, he loved to sit on the kitchen floor of his aunt's home and hit pots and pans with wooden spoons. Is it any wonder that he became a drummer instead of a pianist? He was born with a very high IQ. It is only natural then, that he excels in fields where only super-intelligent minds can function. He's not sure whether his keen mind is a burden or a gift. His extraordinary abilities don't make him any happier. Quite the contrary; sometimes he wishes he were a gas-station mechanic, with average intelligence and a taste for ordinary beer, who loves to go hunting, fishing, and watch the New York Giants on television every Sunday. It will never be.

Zachary squeezes two drops of PowZak into a glass of water. He drinks the water, then uses the compound A antidote to clean the eyedropper and the glass. He decides to further test the relationship between his thoughts and the physical manifestations of those thoughts. His experiment is to see what force fields are generated by the thoughts themselves. Can he actually get an electrical measurement? He wishes he were back in the lab at IBX. He has constructed a makeshift, sensitive galvanometer and wires himself to test the theory. He focuses his thoughts outward toward the floor lamp and pins the needle on the meter. It smokes before it burns out. At the same time, the lamp moves two feet further away from the chair.

"Okay, there's measureable current here," he says aloud in an understatement and swallows hard, amazed at his ability to move the lamp. He observes his reflection and sees no changes. He has a video camera running to record the experiment, and moves his floor lamp back into position next to the chair. Zachary detaches the electrodes from his skin and concentrates on moving a book. With his thoughts, he lifts it from his desk, makes it fly through the air and into his hand, all while sitting in his easy chair. He opens his hand and returns the book through the air to the same spot on his desk.

Next, he gets up from the chair, removes five books from his library, and stacks them on the corner of his desk. He sits back down and again concentrates on moving the books. This time he makes them rotate in a perfect parabolic orbit above his head. He slows them down so the movement is only a few inches per minute. He then speeds them up. He gets them to spin so fast that they make a rustling sound like a large window-fan. He wills a slower speed and stops the two middle books, leaving the outside three spinning. He then makes the outside three stop and spins the inside two in the opposite direction. Then he changes the angle of their orbit to forty-five degrees, to seventy-five degrees, and back to a horizontal plane. He returns the books to his desk. He makes each book move and hover just in front of his face so he can read the title. Without getting up, he returns each to its proper place on his library shelves. He shuts off the video recorder. He again observes his reflection and there is no change.

How much weight can he lift? How far can he make an object travel? He remembers the law of physics: *For every action, there is an equal and opposite reaction.* Zachary is waiting for some symptom of a side effect, or a negative change. He noticed that his sense of smell is keener than it was before he accidentally turned himself into a dog. My God! The very thought of that makes him shake. He assumes there will be a downside to the positive changes, but he doesn't know what form it will take.

Zachary is staring out his living room window at Bay Road. He sees a couple walking their black Labrador retriever. They have a plastic bag with them to pick up the dog droppings and are obviously good neighbors. The bag is loosely tied to the leash and the dog is walking behind the couple. The bag breaks free and Zachary thinks, *The doggy bag dropped; you'd better pick it up.* Both the man and the woman stop cold, then she turns around and picks up the bag. They both look toward the house, then at each other. They shrug their shoulders and continue walking.

Zachary can send messages to other people's minds.

«««◊»»»

The Warrens have a tradition. They always attend the presidential debates in New Hampshire. This year they have a special significance for Daphne because they are being held at her alma mater, Dartmouth College. Although Zachary is essentially apolitical, Daphne is a rabid Democrat. She sees it as her duty to scope out the enemy. She always volunteers for every fund-raiser, and worked tirelessly to get President Obama elected. This Republican debate promises to be interesting. As yet, there is no clear-cut favorite for the nomination.

Emma and Ethan are staying with the Pettersens. They always enjoy sleeping in their grandparents' home because they play billiards. Occasionally the family cat jumps on the pool table to chase the balls, much to the delight of the kids, but Dr. Pettersen cringes because he doesn't want Fellini to scratch the felt. Zachary and Daphne will return to pick them up the following morning at eleven, after spending the night in Hanover.

"Good evening, ladies and gentlemen, and welcome to Dartmouth College." A short introduction follows for each participant. They welcome Bachman, Cain, Huntsman, Paul, Perry, Romney, and Santorum. They all flash plastic smiles and are eager for their few hours of fame.

"The moderators for tonight's debate are Charlie Rose, *Post* political correspondent Karen Tumulty, and *Bloomberg TV* White House correspondent Julianna Goldman. As most of you already know, tonight we will devote this entire debate to the economy. We want to explore the candidates' specific plans for recovery. The nation faces high unemployment, a high deficit, weak growth, and a possible double-dip recession. What will you do differently? Mr. Rose will ask the first question."

"Thank you very much and welcome all. We'll get right to it. Governor Romney, you have been quoted in Iowa as saying that corporations are people. Do you believe they have the same rights as an American citizen?"

Daphne squeezes Zachary's hand and flashes him a mischievous grin in anticipation of Romney's answer. Zachary looks straight up at the ceiling and has a memory. He bought some old VHS tapes of *Andy's Gang* at a garage sale. This was a kids' TV show that aired in the late fifties. Before Ethan was born, when Emma was five or six, she would watch the program. Every time Froggy the Gremlin would be introduced by Andy Devine, he would say, "Plunk your magic twanger, Froggie." You would hear a boing sound, and in a puff of smoke Froggy would appear and croak, "Hiya kids, hiya, hiya." Then Andy would introduce an expert, usually Pasta Fazooli, played by Vito Scotti. Pasta would lecture on some subject, and Froggy would cause poor Pasta to do and say silly things. Zachary remembers the Mad Lib game they played, and the random nouns that got inserted in the blanks. Froggy would do the same thing to his guests. Pasta would say, "You take the whipped cream and..." Then Froggy would interrupt and say, "Squirt it in your face." Pasta would do exactly what Froggy said, then say "Oooh, looka what you maka me do!" Emma must have watched that show a dozen times and laughed every time.

Romney finishes speaking, and the debate continues with a question from Karen Tumulty for the next candidate. He answers, "It is my belief that President Obama has this country on the wrong course. If I'm elected President, instead of spending money on bottomless entitlement programs, I will concentrate on.......making sure the one percent has proper nutrition. For years the poor have had Meals on Wheels deliver food to their doors. It's their turn to return the favor. I will insist that Congress pass legislation that foods be prepared and delivered by poor people to every mansion in America. These foods must have a high concentration of the three most important ingredients to good health: neo-flabby oils, mohair, and Lichtensteins."

Holy shit, it worked! Zachary is delighted.

"You can't be serious," another candidate interjects. "That's the most ridiculous thing I've ever heard. Although I agree that entitlement programs such as Social Security and Medicare must be cut if we are to meet our financial obligations, the emphasis of *where* these funds are used is of most importance, and is not a laughing matter. Right now there is a crisis of leadership, especially in the Democrat-controlled Senate. When we trim entitlement funds, the money should be redirected to.......my sexual harassment defense fund. I'm going to need every cent I can get my hands on to pay off these bimbos."

The audience gasps.

"I don't believe what I'm hearing," a third candidate says with a flabbergasted look. "America has given much to the people of the world. The poem on the Statue of Liberty reads, "Give me your tired, your poor, your huddled masses yearning to breathe free, the wretched refuse of your teeming shore. Send these, the homeless, tempest-tost to me, I lift my lamp beside the golden door!" and.......unfortunately that's exactly what the world has done. Now we are a country of foreigners who don't speak English and rattle on in their native gibberish, while they steal everything they can grab. If I'm elected president, I'll send all the spics, niggers, wetbacks, dagos, and kikes back to where they came from."

The audience is outraged, and they boo and hiss.

"What did you just say? Those are racist comments that have no place in Republican politics, or anywhere in our great country. You should be ashamed of yourself. You don't speak for our party, I can assure you of that. You will never get the chance to serve the people. I've learned one thing from living in middle America. The people are.......indeed in the middle. Did you know that Ohio is the only state in the Union that is round at both ends and high in the middle? Get it? Round at both ends and "hi" in the middle? Did you know that there are many rich people on the Atlantic Coast? In one state everyone wears a New Jersey. What did Della wear? That's what Della wore. Get it? What did Della wear? Did you know there was a song about that?"

The audience laughs, and some roll their programs into balls and throw them on the stage.

Chapter Seven

The Warren family doesn't usually eat out on Wednesday night, but today is Emma's fourteenth birthday. They told her she could do anything she wanted. She could have a big or small party, she could have a few friends over, or she could do nothing at all. She chose to invite her best friends, Carol and Jennifer, and to eat with the family at The Windjammer, her favorite restaurant. When Daphne told Zachary what Emma wanted, he punched the air with his fist and said a loud "Yes!"

Emma is really loving the drama club and has been using an old, heavy camera to film her own skits. They bought her a sleek new SONY video recorder with separate accessory microphones and spotlights. It took her all of fifteen minutes to learn how they work, and she is busy sticking the camera in everyone's face. She brings it to the restaurant and is filming her friends pick up broccoli with the serving tongs. They decide to do a class project called, what else, Salad Bar.

"They love it here, go figure," Zachary says as the three girls fill big white plates while they walk along the thirty-foot glass serving bar. "Most kids don't like vegetables, but these girls are half rabbit, and I think it's great," Daphne says. "Whoever heard of a fourteen-year-old girl who asks for artichokes and asparagus?"

"Hello, Dr. Warren." A gray-haired man, sharply dressed, has walked over to their table. "Forgive the intrusion, but I was going to call you tomorrow. I'm glad I ran into you here." Zachary looks at Daphne. "Daphne, this is James Carlson, the head of R & D at IBX. Mr. Carlson, my wife Daphne. This will have to wait," Zachary says with annoyance. "We have my daughter's birthday to celebrate and..."

"I know. I'm sorry to intrude, but there's something you should know. We are now fully aware that all the original research on the blood pressure drug is yours. We fired your boss on Monday. I am no longer the head of R & D. I'm now senior vice president in charge of all product development. I would like to offer you my old job. I would like you to run the department. We want you to lead an expanded R & D team, and we're keeping research right here in Vermont. I promise it will be very lucrative. That's all I have to say. If you are interested, we can talk some more tomorrow. Nice to have met you, Daphne. Please wish your daughter a happy birthday. Good evening, Zachary."

With that succinct announcement, James Carlson rejoins his party of three sitting on the other side of the room.

Zachary quickly does a balance sheet in his mind. He has the ability to sort through details and reach a decision based on facts and logic. After he decides what is logically correct, he then allows his emotions their due input. He reasons that, while developing PowZak, he will need frequent trips out of state, and he will have a difficult time using the university labs without some overseeing. If he accepts the IBX job, he will have a carte blanche to use the best lab in the country. He can use their equipment for tests that he would have done alone at home, thereby making the process much safer. But the losses are great. He will have less time to spend with his family. Daphne can sense some of what he is thinking by analyzing his body language. Zachary's face is instantly readable to her. She knows by even a slight quiver of his upper lip what he will most likely say next.

"I know you are going to take the job, and I know you have mixed feelings about it. You will be making much more money, which is good for the family, but you will be spending less time with us when our relationship has never been better. You've probably processed all this with your built-in high-speed computer, and reached the same conclusion. I'll say just one thing. Your new job doesn't mean that you will lose any of the precious ground you have reclaimed. You can empower Em to act on her own behalf and to look out for Ethan. When you are home, it will be quality time. I have to work. I know you hate to be home when I'm at school, and we will spend about the same amount of time together as we do now."

Zachary gives Daphne a huge kiss and knocks over a glass of water onto his lap. Emma films them kissing, and the patrons at the other tables are enjoying the spectacle. Ethan looks at his father. "Dad peed his pants! Dad peed his pants!"

"Shut up, dildo!" Emma says as she films him sticking out his tongue at her. "I'm putting all this on YouTube."

«««◊»»»

Daphne is five-foot-seven, was captain of the Dartmouth Nordic Ski team, and practices yoga daily. She has natural blonde hair and hazel eyes. She isn't particularly curvy, but as Spencer Tracy said about Katherine Hepburn, "There ain't much meat on her, but what's there is choice." She is the diametric opposite of Zachary in that she can concentrate on one item indefinitely without distraction. Lately, she has been having an extra glass or two of wine at dinner. She finds it necessary to turn off her brain. She is always studying her family, and she constantly reads them.

Daphne has very recently realized that she has the ability to feel what others are feeling. She has done some of her own research, and it has told her that she is blessed and cursed with the gift of empathy. She is chemically and biologically different from those who do not possess the gift. When you involve yourself in another person's welfare, you activate your own neuronal network in the very same area. It could be happiness, pain, exasperation, envy, fear, or a host of other emotions. When she observes these emotions in others, she feels them herself.

In the past, she had been conducting her life with a symbolic blindfold on and hearing protectors in place to protect her from the sensory overload of receiving too much information. This had made her short-tempered, and many times she appeared uncaring, but she was feeling the pain of others. In fact, she cared *too* much and had to dilute her emotions by turning away.

Daphne has opened the box and let the genie out. She can no longer put the blindfold on. How did Zachary know what Emma would do when he asked her to share the drugs with Ethan? At the Republican debate, she could feel the energy flowing from him. When she touched his hand she felt an electric tingle, just like when you walk across a carpeted floor and touch a metal door knob. She could sense his mischievous delight just before each of the candidates spoke. He was chortling like a boy, and she like a girl, and they had a wonderful time goofing on them. They went back to their motel room and made love by candlelight. She could not remember a happier day, except when her children were born. She suspects that Zachary has tremendous power, but has no idea what it is.

My vision is incredible. I can see all around me, and my reflexes are instantaneous. I can jump in any direction and make turns that no jet pilot could ever contemplate. Zachary thinks as he sits on the edge of the curtain rod above the kitchen window. He ponders evolution and the special niche into which each life form has evolved. *The biggest threat of all is man,* he theorizes while he sits in the sunlight enjoying the aroma of the compost that has just been ground under the sink.

We think we're so special. Ah yes, the intelligent creature. Zachary has read about Koko the gorilla. She knows over 1,000 signs and recognizes even more spoken words. He knows that man isn't the only tool-using animal. Sea otters use rocks from the ocean floor. They put them on their chests as they float on the surface, catch shellfish, and crack them open on the rocks. Chimps use sticks to open termite mounds. Elephants dig holes to look for water, and when they find some, they strip bark from a tree to stuff it in the hole so the water doesn't evaporate. They then return to the same hole for another drink.

Is not the greatest life form that which will survive? Man will go the way of the carrier pigeon. A single-cell bacteria will endure after all else is gone. *Long live bacteria,* he muses, rubbing his front legs together.

"Uh oh, horsefly," Daphne says and reaches for the Raid. Zachary quickly zooms out of the kitchen, down the hall, and into his study. Daphne is right behind him, but before she enters the room, Zachary morphs back into himself. He shows her a dead fly which he had previously killed in the event anyone saw him.

"Friend of yours?" he asks Daphne holding the fly on a half-sheet of note paper. *I feel like a murderer.*

"How did you catch him?"

"I have fast hands."

"Not that fast. What did you do, just snag him out of the air as he flew into the room?"

"Fly's dead."

"So I see. Nicely done. Thanks." Daphne looks over her shoulder as she walks away. Zachary lunges and pinches her bottom as she reaches the door.

"See, fast hands. Oops, I dropped my fly."

"Is that an invitation?"

"Now that you mention it." Zachary grabs Daphne and carries her into the bedroom. They shut the door and make love before dinner. They make love again after dinner.

"At this rate, I'm going to be pregnant."

"Oh my God, I never thought of that!"

"And you're a scientist?" Daphne says as she puts her cold feet on Zachary's legs. "Oh nuts, we have therapy tomorrow night."

"Daffy, we don't have to do this anymore. You know that."

"I know it, but they need us. I feel sorry for them. They obviously aren't getting along, at least not physically."

"Wait a minute, let me get this straight. I'm only a dumb scientist. They are considered the premier marriage counselors in New England, highly recommended by your mother, so we pay them $250 for fifty minutes, right?"

"Right."

"And it's our job to save *their* marriage?"

"I bought that video from Florence Saturday."

"Whatever for? Daffy, why are you patronizing her?"

"Do you want to watch it?" Daphne asks.

"Why not?" Zachary puts the DVD in the player, and they watch the sex video prepared by Norma and William Merchant. Everything about the video is funny. From the opening credits to the soft misty lighting, breathy voices, and fake orgasms. The soundtrack is some kind of synthesized harp music that plays over and over in a loop.

"Shit, this will put us off sex for years."

They laugh so loudly that they wake up Ethan. Emma has her headphones on, so she doesn't hear the ruckus. Ethan knocks on their door.

"Come in."

"What's so funny? Can I watch the movie?"

Zachary quickly turns off the DVD player with the remote, and the TV pops back on with PBS News Hour. "It wasn't a movie. There was a funny story on the news, little buddy."

"What was it?"

Emma sees Ethan walk by, takes off her headphones, and walks into her parents' bedroom. "Em, they heard a funny story on the news and they're going to tell us what it was." Ethan is excited.

Zachary says, "There was this man who had a pet chimpanzee that he walked on a special harness. He took it to the mall in....er...Chicago, but the chimp, called Snuggie, became agitated with all the people around. So the chimp went berserk and took off all his master's clothes. The poor man was running naked through the mall, chasing after the chimp, which was dragging his pants behind and shrieking with delight."

Emma spots the DVD jacket with the blurry sexual image, and this provokes a fit of uncontrollable laughter. Ethan sees

Emma laughing, so he also laughs, although Zachary's story wasn't really that funny.

"Em, would you escort Ethan back to bed? And if you say anything to him, I will kill you," Daphne whispers in her ear.

Emma laughs again when she returns to their room after putting Ethan to bed. She holds out her hand. "You owe me. Give."

Zachary sheepishly grins and hands her the DVD. "This is so badly done we couldn't stop laughing. There is nothing in here that will shock you, and I doubt you will learn anything either."

"Did you get it from your therapists?"

"Yes, we did."

"You don't need them anymore."

"See Daffy, I told you. Em's got it nailed."

"Don't call me Daffy. Em, please don't try any of that stuff until you're at least thirty-five, and don't show it to your friends. If it gets back to the Sidtherns, we'll be embarrassed."

"I'm going to put it on YouTube. Love you guys."

"No, bad idea. Give it back, Em," Daphne says.

Zachary has been experimenting with an alternate delivery system for PowZak. It's such a powerful drug that much smaller quantities will also yield surprising results. With a minute amount, 200 to 400 percent increases in energy will result. For example, if a person can lift 100 pounds over his or her head, by ingesting a small dose of PowZak that would then increase to 200 to 400 pounds. That is a multiple that can be roughly used in any activity. If a person can remember a paragraph with 50 words, that person will then be able to memorize a paragraph with 200 words. All physical and mental activity will respond to what Zachary has written and formulated as a micro-dose. It is not powerful enough to cause any permanent physical changes. Fifty micro-doses would have to be combined to achieve the results he can get with two drops of PowZak. He can also administer a micro-dose to others, in carefully controlled experiments.

He has been working in his basement shop for a week to fabricate a small atomizer that he converted from one of Daphne's discarded perfume bottles. He created an ingenious screw-top with a polymer glue that lets no air in or out. He put a small stainless steel spring and miniature washer in place under the squeeze top to restrict the up and down movement.

The end result is that one squirt from his custom atomizer equals one micro-dose of PowZak. He now has a travel kit to take with him. Since the small perfume bottle is glass, he carries it in a shockproof container that he can slip in his pants pocket. It will not be poured into another container, such as a drinking glass, so he doesn't need to have the compound A antidote standing by to rinse the glass.

He wanted to perfect the micro-dose because he doesn't want to fear morphing into an unwanted shape. He still doesn't have total control over the changling process. If he hadn't taken two drops of compound A after Daphne followed the fly back to his study, he could have been in big trouble. He keeps the antidote in small vials that have been strategically hidden in his study, his workshop, and even his car. If he hadn't taken the antidote before carrying her into their bedroom, there's no telling what might have happened when his mind encountered the earthy aromas of love-making. Daphne did not need to see Zachary Taylor Warren, Superfly.

He has agreed to take over the R & D department at IBX, and he starts work in two weeks. They have hired four other researchers, and the total staff is now 125 people, including interdepartmental administrative support.

He wonders how he can incorporate PowZak into the formulary. It can be combined with the existing IBX drugs to make them more effective. There has been so much adverse publicity about stem-cell research, biologically altered grains, and animal cloning. I don't know what PowZak can do. Do I dare? I can see it now. He remembers the Edward Randall story and what Louise said. He now has a real-world drug that is not a fantasy.

I guess Louise would say, "Add it to Viagra. Your penis will stay hard for two and a half years. Add it to nasal spray, and not only will it clear your sinuses, you'll be able to smell your neighbors private parts a quarter of a mile away. Add it to LSD..."

No, PowZak must never be brought to market in any form, even as an enhancement to an existing drug. What if I took four drops instead of two, or an entire teaspoon full? What would then happen? That's the trouble. No matter who is testing the drug, they will try to reach its limits. What if I took a tablespoon full and then willed myself to disappear? Would I be transported into another dimension?

He remembers the old novelty song from 1950 that he heard recently on a PBS music nostalgia show.

THE THING
Recorded by Phil Harris
Written by Charles Grean

While I was walking down the beach
one bright and sunny day
I saw a great big wooden box a-floatin' in the bay
I pulled it in and opened it up and much to my surprise
Oh! I discovered a (boom-boom-boom) right before my eyes

95

Oh! I discovered a (boom-boom-boom) right before my eyes

(The poor guy tries to get rid of The Thing. He takes it to a junk dealer, his wife, a hobo on the street, and finally Saint Peter, and everybody turns him away. He's stuck with The Thing for good.)

The moral of this story is if you're out on the beach
And you should see a great big box and it's within your reach
Don't ever stop and open it up - that's my advice to you
'Cause you'll never get rid of the (boom-boom-boom) no matter what you do
Oh, you'll never get rid of the (boom-boom-boom) no matter what you do.

Chapter Eight

Zachary took a micro-dose of PowZak before he and Daphne left for their therapy session. They are now sitting in the waiting room. With all his perceptions heightened fourfold, he hears a faintly audible whirring sound. He looks up and sees a small glass circle in the corner of the ceiling and spots a lens that has just zoomed to its wide-angle setting. He quickly takes out a pen and writes on the little spiral notepad he keeps in his pocket.

"Don't look up; they have a camera here in the ceiling. They are probably recording everything we say."

Daphne turns red and tries to control her anger. He puts the notepad back in his pocket.

"Zachary, why do you have to bring home a different sexual partner every week? Last week it was those obese twins. The week before it was that ghastly, weird, six-foot-three-inch transvestite massage therapist. This week it's that cute little dancer who loves high heels. I must admit, he *is* sweet. I didn't know you were a bisexual. At least you're including me in all the fun."

"You're welcome, Daphne. Where did I hear that, right after Christmas, the Sidtherns will be vacationing at a nudist colony in the British Virgin Islands? Perhaps we can tag along with them and make some new group sex videos. I wonder if they're into S & M like we are. I'll bet Florence can be a hot little number with a few Pina Coladas in her. Should we mention the idea now or wait until next session?"

"Let's wait; the timing has to be perfect."

"Hello Daphne, hello Zachary, and how are you on this fine Tuesday evening?" Florence's outward appearance is bubbly as she walks into the waiting room, but she has deep circles under her eyes. As they enter the therapy room, Mitchell is as usual, except that he holds a white Styrofoam cup of coffee. He puts his left hand over his mouth to hide a yawn that sneaks out.

Zachary senses two things. He remembers the familiar aroma of the coffee and also detects the faint aroma of confectioners' sugar. The coffee, and what was apparently pastry of some kind are from Dunkin' Donuts. There's a shop in front of the Champlain Motel, which is quite far from the Sidtherns' home. Could Mitchell be staying at the motel after a dispute with Florence? The third, and perhaps most important piece of information, is that there are two other cars in the parking lot in addition to the Warren's BMW. The Sidtherns must have driven here separately. So far the evidence is strictly circumstantial, but neither of the therapists will acknowledge the other's presence.

"Did you watch the video?" Florence asks as Mitchell holds his fountain pen at the ready above his clipboard.

"We've reached a new phase in our relationship, Florence. We are physically close at all times. I don't intend on being any more graphic than that. Zachary and I are once again a loving couple. I'll bet you want to know what turned things around for us."

"Please, tell me. I would like to know."

"Peanut butter," Zachary responds before Daphne can speak. "We both love peanut butter spread around our private parts. We were using this really chunky kind without much oil, but we switched to a smooth peanut butter with gobs of peanut oil, and we lick it all off. The only problem we have is the maid now has to change the sheets daily."

"I didn't know you had a maid."

"That's not the point, Florence," Mitchell says with annoyance. "The point is they really don't need that dumb video any more than we do."

"What *do* we need, Mitchell dear, besides separate lives in separate houses? I might as well tell the two of you that

Mitchell and I are having a trial separation. Since we have been seeing each other constantly day and night, there has been too much friction. The choice was to live together and work separately, or work together and live separately. Since Mitchell loves money more than he loves me, we decided to work together and live separately." Florence is ready for battle.

"I'm going to end this session early, and we will not charge you," Mitchell says calmly. He is pressing down so hard on his clipboard that the fountain pen ink has run down the page and onto his left pants leg. "I'm glad that the two of you have rekindled your physical relationship. That part wasn't easy, but it will be even more difficult to sustain it. The problems that brought you here in the first place must be resolved, or there is a high danger of the same thing happening again. You must continue to explore those issues, and it will take time to dig them all out. There are gender issues, issues of trust, power issues, and others as well. So, by all means be happy with your triumph, but know that careful planning is necessary for continued success."

"You sound like a landscape salesman who wants to sell us grass-cutting services even though it will soon be winter, and there is no need for your caution. Sometimes life and love *can* be simple," Zachary says.

"It's never simple. There are simple truths, I will grant you that, but when you add a man and a woman into the equation, those simple truths often turn into simple nightmares. See you in three weeks, and I guarantee by then we will project a united front and complete professionalism."

As the Warrens reach their car, they can clearly hear Florence shouting, "Money, money, money, money!" over and over.

"I think they're going to need a bit of work, Daphne. Are you sure you're up to it?"

"I must admit that Mitchell does have a point," Daphne says. "We do have to be careful. I don't want to go back to the way things were."

"Then we won't. I believe it's that simple, Daffy."

"Don't call me Daffy, or I'll call you Zak, Zak!"

«««◊»»»

Zachary hates to be called Zack, whether it's spelled Zack, Zak, or Zach. He much prefers his full name. Of course, Daphne knows this. When she calls him Zak, she knows that his emotions will be aroused. In their present state of constant physical agitation, this has once again led them to their bedroom. Emma and Ethan are watching television, and their parents say a quick hello before disappearing. With his heightened awareness, the lovemaking is incredible. Next time he is going to squirt a micro-dose of PowZak into Daphne's drink and see what that does when they go to bed.

It is Wednesday morning at nine. Everyone is at school, and Zachary is in his study. Ten days from now he will return to IBX. He's planning experiments to further determine the limits of PowZak. He wants to quantify cell-growth rates, as observed with the Titan electron microscope. He hopes that he can extend the data outward with computer simulation. How heavy an object can he lift with a micro-dose, two micro-doses, two drops, a teaspoonful, a tablespoonful, an ounce? He has a rough idea, based on his primitive real-life approximations. Two micro-doses equal about 500 pounds. There are 50 micro-doses in two drops. That's 25,000 pounds. There are 120 drops in a teaspoon. That's 120 divided by 2, equals 60 x 25,000 pounds. That's 1,500,000 pounds. There are six teaspoons in an ounce. So, theoretically, if he drank one ounce of PowZak, he would be able to lift 9,000,000 pounds using his physical strength. Telekinesis is another matter. How much weight could he move with his thoughts after drinking two drops of PowZak is yet to be determined.

"Faster than a speeding bullet. More powerful than a locomotive. Able to leap tall buildings in a single bound. Look! Up in the sky! It's a bird! It's a plane! It's...Zachary Taylor Warren," he says, leaping onto his desk. He postulates that everything can be extrapolated with the same degree of increase. For instance, if he can run at ten miles per hour, by taking an ounce of PowZak he would be then able to run at 150,000 miles per hour carrying 9,000,000 pounds. And if he drank a full glass, say 16 ounces, and the multiples increased exponentially, he would be able to do some serious shit. He would be able to hit a baseball from Vermont to South Africa, assuming it would stay together and not burn up in the atmosphere.

In Randall's story, Ralph was a real jerk. The first thing he thought about was rubbing PowZak on his penis. The second thing was fixing his dented car fender. The third thing, just before it was stolen, was going to be his attempt to clone money. He was cheating on his wife, and in the end he got what he deserved. He was no more able to handle the power of the drug than he was able to control the most insignificant parts of his life. Zachary questions whether he is any different. He was actually contemplating squirting a micro-dose into Daphne's drink before they went to bed. What if she didn't realize her own strength and did damage to herself or the children? What if she became frightened of her heightened awareness and it severely traumatized her? Was he seriously considering this to satisfy his own sexual curiosity?

He remembered Lord Acton's quote, written in 1887. *Power tends to corrupt, and absolute power corrupts absolutely. Great men are almost always bad men.* Another Englishman, William Pitt, said something similar in his speech to the House of Lords in 1770: *Unlimited power is apt to corrupt the minds of those who possess it.* There is no question that with PowZak, Zachary Warren has absolute power. He takes a teaspoonful and walks outside on the deck facing Lake Champlain.

The majestic soaring of seagulls has always been a visual treat to Zachary. He loves to watch them weave and dive into the water. Their pure white bodies with black wing tips make them one of nature's most beautiful sights. When the sun is setting over the Adirondacks, the birds are lit from below and glow golden against the sky. When there are gray clouds overhead, the highlighted birds look positively electric against the gunmetal blackness above.

Zachary pushes off the deck railing and soars to fourteen hundred feet above the water. He has all his human senses, and he has the ability to fly. He sees some red-tailed hawks riding thermals close to the shoreline. He's traveling much too high and fast for them to be a threat. He hears a loud, intrusive roar and spots two F-16s from the Vermont Air National Guard flying close together above the lake, about one mile from the New York shore. He increases his speed and flies right above the trailing jet. He's one foot above the pilot's canopy and matches the jet in all its movements.

"Holy shit, Captain, I've got a bird directly above, and he's keeping up with me."

"Say what, Lieutenant? Please repeat."

"Sir, I've got a God damned bird flying above me."

"Lieutenant, we're flying at 280 knots. What the hell are you talking about?"

Zachary breaks away from the wingman's plane and moves into the same position above the captain's plane.

"Lieutenant, there's a seagull flying over my fucking head. I thought you were nuts; now I think I'm nuts. Activate your camera."

"I already have. I've got it, Sir."

"Hello, Control Tower, we are increasing speed to mach one and proceeding north on heading 920. Acknowledge."

"Roger, Air Force 24."

At mach one, Zachary easily stays with the fighter jets. He zooms ahead of them and does loops around both planes.

"Captain, this is Control Tower, Burlington Airport."

"Go ahead."

"We detect a small unidentified flying object on our radar that is traveling with you. Is that in your view?

"Yes, it is."

"What is the object?"

"That's classified at this time, Control Tower."

Zachary breaks away from the formation and soars into the upper atmosphere at mach ten. He then returns to the surface of the lake and dives down to three hundred feet beneath the waves. The lieutenant continues to film the spot where the bird disappeared beneath the water. Suddenly the seagull flies straight up out of the lake directly toward the captain's jet and lands on its nose. Zachary folds his wings like any normal seagull would do when sitting atop a sailboat's boom. He then breaks away, loops backwards, and returns to the railing on his deck. He spots a large minnow swimming near the shore and swallows it. *Um, delicious.* When the jets are out of sight, he morphs back into his human form.

»»»«»«««

At the same time Daphne arrives home with the children, four cars with flashing blue lights also arrive at the Warren home. Zachary sees FBI written on two of the vehicles, so he quickly uses his powers to change the computer disks with the PowZak information into two paper clips that he shoves into his desk drawer. The vials of compound A are also changed into paper clips.

"What's going on, Mom? Is Dad all right?"

"Zachary!" Daphne screams. He runs out and hugs his family. "I'm fine, what's going on here?"

"I'm Special Agent Washington, and this is Special Agent Krugman, FBI. We'd like to talk to you, Sir, Ma'am."

"What's this about?" Daphne asks, looking fearfully at Zachary.

"I have no idea. Why are armed men standing in our driveway, and what exactly do you want from my family?"

"We have a search warrant for the premises, and I order all of you to remain outside while we conduct the search."

"What the hell for? You have no right!" Daphne screams.

The FBI agents do not tell the Warrens specifically why they are searching the premises. All they say is "suspicion of terrorist activity." After conducting their search using various infra-red and electrical scanners, they invite the Warrens back into their home.

"Dr. Warren, you are a research scientist, and Mrs. Warren, you are a guidance counselor. We have reason to believe that terrorist activity may have originated from this neighborhood. Doctor, have you been involved with any recent experiments in areas other than your drug research? Are you a member of any alien organization, or do you have contacts with foreign nationals, other than those in Europe who are part of the IBX team?"

"That's totally ridiculous. I have a top-secret government clearance, you moron, and I've worked with the National Security Administration on many projects while at IBX. What the hell kind of terrorist activity? I guarantee you won't find anything in this neighborhood. You have very bad information, and you're scaring my children. Please leave here at once. Where the hell are you going with our computers?"

"We will probably be back to ask you some more questions, so please remain in Shelburne. We will return your computers after a thorough examination. Your neighbors will also be part of this investigation."

Cameras: Zachary had forgotten that the aircraft carry high resolution cameras, and they probably followed his flight back to the deck behind his house. He has put his family at risk. Daphne is livid and asks him to walk with her into the bedroom.

"Zachary, what the hell is going on here? Tell me the God damned truth! You know what's going on, I am certain of that, because I can read you like a God damned book."

"You are correct. There will be a time soon when I can share what I have discovered. You will have to trust me till then."

"No Zachary, that won't do. Trust? You have already violated my trust by not telling me anything till now. Not that you've said what it is you're doing. What is going on? God damn it!"

"I changed myself into a seagull and flew alongside some Air Force jets. I guess it made them nervous. I forgot that they have on-board cameras."

"You are really trying my patience, Zachary. They can put us both in jail for no reason. If you don't tell me what's going on, you can live by yourself. Is that clear enough?"

Daphne paces back and forth at the foot of the bed. She passes too close to the DVD player and knocks it to the floor.

"The dog that sniffed out Em's drugs, the fly that you chased into my study, the seagull that the Air Force traced back to our home, those outrageous things that the Republican candidates said, they are all me. I can change into any shape I want with a new drug I've invented, and I can send my brain waves into others at will."

"What outrageous things? You need help, Zachary. I *thought* our life was too good to be true. My God, I'm living with a raving lunatic."

"When the children are asleep, I want you to come with me into my study. I'll show you what I've done. I was afraid of scaring you, but what's happened is much worse. You must absolutely swear that you will tell no one, not your mother, your father, not our children. No one! If I am to trust you, you must give me your word." Zachary's voice is quivering, and his body is shaking. Daphne has never seen him like this. She knows one of two things is true. Either he's completely insane, or he's telling her the truth.

"You have my word, unless you are going to show me something that will do harm to you, or this family. It seems that it already has. Our home and our privacy have been violated. I will not stand by and let you do any kind of experiments that will do harm, especially to our children. Is that clear? At midnight, you show me what you've done. This had better be good."

Chapter Nine

One week later, Daphne picks up *The Burlington Free Press* from the front steps and reads the lead story on page one. "Zachary, listen to this. Oh my God, they have photographs of Bay Road, and you can even see our house. Do you know the O'Donnell family four houses down? They're hosting an exchange student from Syria. He has been arrested for smuggling explosives with intent to do terrorist activity. The family had no idea. They were just as surprised as I am. The FBI solved the case two days ago. No wonder there was so much activity. Oh look, there's a great photograph of you on page two of the business section. It says Zachary Taylor Warren has been named the new head of IBX Research and Development. They have a short bio and mention me and the kids. Look, we're famous. What do you think of that student, right here on our street?"

"He's a sleazebag who should be executed for treason. Let me see my photo. They didn't get my good side."

"You are so vain. By the way, the FBI returned our computers yesterday and didn't erase anything. I didn't set yours up because I know you will want to. Agent Washington thanked us for our cooperation and gave Em and Ethan FBI baseball caps."

"Screw the FBI. Daphne, my car is being serviced at ten, and they need to hold it overnight. Seems I burned out the clutch. They always take forever, so I'll drive you and the kids to school in your car and pick you up at the end of the day. I need to run some errands, if that's all right with you."

"That's fine, but don't forget, you have an appointment at seven-thirty. You promised, so don't plan on anything else."

Zachary drops his family off, Ethan at the elementary school, Em and Daphne at the middle school. *She looks so tired. I've put her through some hard times.*

Zachary is sitting on the edge of his bed. He's in fine shape and has always had a flat stomach. He notices segmented ridges that are three times wider than his normal abs. *They sort of look like an insect's thorax but with human skin.*

He laughs to himself. *I do hit myself with electric charges every time I take a large dose of PowZak. They say that cockroaches will inherit the Earth in the event of a nuclear war because they can absorb the most radiation. Perhaps I'm turning into a giant cockroach, just like poor Gregor Samsa. I'll definitely lose points with Daphne in bed.*

"What a boring car," Zachary says out loud as he picks up Ethan. "How was school today, little buddy?"

"Fine."

"Did you do anything of interest that you would like to share?"

"No."

"If you had to pick any subject that you could take, all by itself, without any of the others, what would it be?"

"I don't know."

Zachary pulls into the middle school parking lot. Daphne is surrounded by six fourteen-year-olds who are mobbing Emma. They give her high-fives, a few hugs, and go to their respective buses and parents' cars.

"They had a scrimmage today between the junior varsity and the varsity soccer teams. Guess what?" Daphne says excitedly.

"No way." Zachary responds. "They won?"

"Em scored all three goals. Nobody could catch her, and she wove in and out down the field like a hot knife through butter. She couldn't be stopped. The entire school is buzzing about her speed."

Oh shit, did I not rinse my glass with compound A after I gave myself the last dose? If I put it on the kitchen counter, and Em grabbed it to pour herself a glass of water, there could have been trace elements of PowZak. That would be enough to speed her up.

Zachary quickly runs into the kitchen. *No, everything is fine. I put it in the dishwasher.*

"Dad, that dog is back," Emma shouts from the living room. A large German shepherd is standing on the Warren's back deck, looking in through the sliding glass door. Zachary walks into the living room, and the dog disappears around the side of the house.

«««‹›»»»

"You don't have to drive me, Daphne. I would have gone exactly as I promised."

"We have only one car today, and I don't like to be stranded at home without transportation. You never know if there will be an emergency. See you in an hour."

Zachary walks into a room not unlike his own living room, except that there are more paintings on the walls. There are three sets of double chairs, and magazines are neatly placed on a coffee table that also holds linzer cookies and Italian nut tarts. There is coffee brewing, and the aroma is too much for him to resist. He pours a cup and grabs a nut tart. Ten minutes later a short, round man greets him. He is bald except for bushy gray hair above each ear and at the back of his head, and he has a genuinely infectious smile.

"Welcome to my world. If you think you have trouble now, wait until you get my bill. I'm Antonio Principo, MD, PHD, I play DVDs, and I wear BVDs."

They shake hands. The psychiatrist notices that Zachary's palm is sweaty, and he talks about the paintings in the waiting room to put him at ease. "That's an original copy of a Cezanne. My wife painted it. I bought most of these in Boston. Twenty years ago they were supposed to be up and coming artists. Unfortunately, I believe most of them came and went. Wadayagonna do? I have a good collection of ancient oil lamps. Come on inside, I'll show you what I mean."

Dr. Principo leads Zachary into a cluttered office. There are art objects piled everywhere. His oil lamp collection is displayed on two large shelves on either side of the bay window that overlooks his garden. His entire desk surface is similarly cluttered with papers, small pieces of sculpture, old Lionel train cabooses, and a small brass pocket trumpet sitting on its bell. It reminds Zachary of a photo he saw of Sigmund Freud's study. The doctor's office is in his home in the town of Charlotte and overlooks Lake Champlain.

"So I hear from your wife that you're another laker family. It's great to watch the sunset over the Adirondacks, but unfortunately it makes me think. It's supposed to calm me down, but it does the opposite. Wait a minute, I'm not paying you to hear my troubles, you're paying me to hear yours. I'll have to add more time to be fair. As a matter of fact, you're the last person I'm seeing today, so if I ramble on too long just remind me of the time.

"Actually, now that I think of it, I never get to talk about myself. It's a good idea in your case, because you have a highly analytical mind. How can you trust me with intimate details about yourself if I'm an enigma?

"I had a nice talk with Daphne, and she is concerned about you. You know how wives are. But here you are. Does that mean that you agree with her that something's wrong, or are you here just to keep her quiet? I assure you it won't matter either way. There are lots of things to talk about. Naturally, nothing we say leaves this room. I don't use tape recorders. That is a device for lazy people who should be listening to talking books and not dealing face-to-face with other people. So why is Daphne concerned about you?"

"She thinks I'm delusional."

"Whoa, that's a good start. As a matter of fact, it's a roaring, flying start. Delusional, now there's a two-dollar word. Okay, Zachary, can you remember seeing, thinking, or saying anything today that was fantasy and not reality?"

"No."

"God, that was a dumb question. If you are delusional, everything you see would appear real to you whether it is fantasy or reality. I hate labels. Most of them don't fit. Let me put it another way. What is it about your behavior that worries Daphne?"

"Since you talked with her, you already know."

"That is absolutely true, but I want to hear it from you. Actually, Daphne and I met a couple of times. We both thought it was a good idea."

"How many times?"

"A couple, three."

"Three? A kinky couple."

"Yes, a kinky couple. Remember, Zachary, there are always four sides to everything. In this case, there's her truth, your truth, the truth as I see it, and the actual truth that probably bears no resemblance to any of the other three. So what gives?" Dr. Principo holds up his hand, telling Zachary not to answer. He runs into the waiting room, grabs two nut tarts, and brings them back on a paper napkin. "Sorry, I got hungry, go ahead."

"What else did she tell you?"

"She told me your parents and twin brother died when you were two years old, and you were raised by your aunt. Were you close physically? Did she hug you, tell you she loved you, that sort of thing?"

"Not much. I suppose she was rather detached, but she put me through Cornell, and left me a tidy sum."

"Through Cornell, with honors no less. You got a Rhodes Scholarship."

"Is there *anything* Daphne hasn't told you? Perhaps she should be in here instead of me."

"Don't be angry with either of us. She's only acting out of love and concern. What we discuss stays in this room. I will not be giving her progress reports of any kind. I made that clear from the very beginning. Let me tell you something. I'm the baddest shrink in the valley for getting to the facts. Naturally, Daphne and you will not see the same event the same way. Remember what I said about different truths. I'm really a clam digger in your vast historical tidal flat, always digging, digging, trying to find the elusive mollusks of reality."

"You use colorful images."

"Colorful schmulerful, life is too short to fill it up with misinformation and dead ends. You're a scientist, you know that. Tell me more about your aunt. Did you do things together?"

"Not much, really. She was probably agoraphobic."

"So, you must have been pretty lonely. Did she ever take you to church?"

"No, never."

"Do you, Daphne and the kids ever go to church?"

"No, religion has never been a part of our lives. I'm anti-religion. Spirituality is another matter. That should be personal and not ritualized. I love Buddhist doctrines."

"I completely agree. My father was Roman Catholic, and my mother was Jewish...why are you smiling?"

"I could tell that you were at least part Jewish by the way you talk."

"Aha, very good. My speech patterns were formed at a very early age. Children absorb so much. Before the age of six, we're like giant sponges. A chance encounter lasting only a few hours can stay with us for the rest of our lives. Your family's death is just one example. Later on in life, we're better able to cope with hardships, unless too much damage has been done and there are no reserves.

"I was brought to the synagogue, was Bah Mitzvahed, and raised Jewish. My mother was deeply religious, but my father didn't care. At first he came to the synagogue, but he quickly stopped going. In the early days, he was basically an Italian anarchist at heart, completely secular and apolitical."

"Were you an only child?"

"Actually, yes, I was. Let me tell you what happened. When my father retired at sixty-five, he decided to become uber-religious. This often happens when people get old and close to death. So both my parents were now uber-religious. The big problem was different religions. They started bickering about who was right. They had me when they were in their mid-thirties. So there I was in Boston, trying to start a practice, and my parents informed me that they no longer loved each other and were getting divorced. For three straight months I got daily calls from both of them. They did finally split. My father died the following year and my mother six months later. As far as I'm concerned, it was religion that killed my parents. Their love for each other should have been more important than those empty prayers they would rattle off."

"Yes, I agree."

"I visited them one Saturday evening. She's in one room reciting in Hebrew, and he's in another room reciting in Latin. Each was trying to drown out the other. So what did I learn from this?"

"Don't force your kids into religion?"

"Exactly! We've raised our daughters without Catholic or Jewish guilt. We decided our family unit was most important. Why am I telling you all this? That was my personal decision. You are now at a point in your life when you must also decide whether or not your family is most important."

"There are things more important than love of family, doctor. Love of Earth has to come first, love of truth."

"Zachary, Zachary, you have no role models, no examples. All you have is your science and your extraordinary intelligence. With the absence of a warm, fuzzy family structure, your books became number one, and they remain so."

Zachary notices the books in Dr. Principo's library. The doctor observes that his gaze is wandering. This is a sign that that their conversation is too intense, and Zachary would soon pull back into self-protection.

"See any books that you like?" The doctor asks as he eats the second nut tart. Zachary can't read all the titles from fifteen feet away, but does see *On Aggression* by Konrad Lorenz, *Emerson's Demanding Optimism* by Gertrude Reif Hughes, and two books by Edward Randall, *The SourSide*, and *Collected Stories*. Dr. Principo has skillfully placed the Randall books so they would be on the right side of the second shelf. He knows that the human eye moves from left to right, and often the greatest visual impact occurs on the lower right.

"I see you also like Edward Randall's *Collected Stories*. No doubt Daphne has told you about PowZak."

"Yes, she told me a lot of things. I know you are now the R & D Director of IBX. Tell me truthfully, are you up to the job? I don't mean ability-wise; I mean how is your emotional state?"

"I can handle it. It will probably be good to concentrate on something large enough to distract me. I discovered a new drug that lowers blood pressure, is anti-anxiety, and produces absolutely no side effects."

"Now you got me interested. No side effects? I would prescribe it like candy. Actually, it's better than candy because refined sugar isn't good for you. When will it be available?"

"They're going to speed up development with a target date of this time next year. We'll be very busy. Did she discuss PowZak?"

"Yes, she said that you mentioned another drug that you discovered. She also said that you told her that you changed into a dog, a fly, a seagull, and that you could transmit thoughts into other people's minds. You also told her that you could move objects. The dog you supposedly changed into showed up on your back deck while you were in the house, it turns out the FBI was not in your neighborhood chasing after a supersonic terrorist seagull, and I have no idea what I can say about the fly. Zachary, if you are able, I would like you to address these issues one at a time. If not, that's okay, too."

"Fucking Bastards International, what right do they have to search our home and confiscate our computers?"

"Never mind, I like the FBI. I've worked with Special Agent Krugman on many occasions as a consultant. They caught a bona fide terrorist who was intent on blowing up a shopping mall. As far as I'm concerned, there is a time for intervention, even if it steps on our toes. I love privacy as much as you do, but would either of us like to be visited by the police telling us that our loved ones had just been killed in an explosion? Tell me about PowZak. Tell me about the seagull. Did you develop this new drug at IBX?"

"I confirmed my research at IBX with their Titan microscope and electronic testing equipment. They have one of the best labs in the world, hard to beat. All the theories were formulated by me offsite in my own study."

"What does this drug do?"

"Basically, it enhances."

"That sounds like Louise in Randall's story. Add a few drops to your aftershave lotion and you'll smell nice. To do the things you claim, it has to be much more than an enhancer. When was the first time you used the drug?"

"I don't remember."

"Of course you do. You keep precise records of everything. I'm not saying you're anal-retentive, but I'll bet you not only know the day, you probably recorded the time, temperature, and what color shirt you were wearing. What you're really telling me is that you're not ready to talk about it. Do you realize what you're asking of me? I feel like I'm watching a science fiction movie. The hero, you, can become invisible, or change into a God-damned bird, or buzz around the house like a horsefly. Talk about willful suspension of disbelief. Look, I'm a scientist just like you are.

"Actually, I'm not going to press you on this because, quite frankly, I don't want to scare you off. All I want is some discussion on PowZak. What do you *want* to tell me? I won't ask any more questions."

"It's about cell regeneration and the spontaneous, planned, predictable growth of electrically stimulated cells. They can be controlled by thought waves and the host body made to follow the exact commands of his or her brain. If the person taking the drug wishes to change into a God-damned bird, that's exactly what will happen to him. He will change into a God-damned bird."

"What form would you most like to assume? A police dog, a seagull, and a horsefly don't sound very exciting. Surely there must be some other changling you could morph into. What else can the drug do? Oops, sorry, that was a question."

"Mental discipline is of the utmost importance. It really doesn't matter what shape is assumed. It's the awareness factor, becoming one with the consciousness of the bird or whatever other creature you change into. PowZak is like a Barlow lens on a telescope. As you know, that lens will double or triple the magnification of whatever eyepiece you are using. PowZak will do the same thing in whatever task the host mind sets for it. For instance, if you want to jump in the air, by regulating the amount of the drug and the electrical stimulation, you can control how high you can jump. If you want to learn a foreign language, and you would normally be able to learn five phrases a day, depending on how much PowZak you took, you could learn the entire language in a matter of days or even hours."

"Very interesting. It's that powerful."

"It's *more* than that powerful. I've yet to probe more than a small fraction of its capability."

"At first you told Daphne that you would show her what the drug would do. When your kids were asleep and you took her into your study, you decided not to. Why?"

"This must be my own quest. It may be too intense even for *me* to handle. How can I inflict the consequences on her?"

"How about me? We're both scientists. Show me some small example of PowZak's power. You shake your head no. I must use some basic philosophical logic now. Since

Daphne questions your stability, and this is a feeling I share, there are only two conclusions that can be reached. The first is that you must provide tangible evidence that your drug will do what you say it will do. The second is that in absence of any tangible proof, you are then suspected of fabricating the evidence. That's why you are here talking to me. I want you to think about not isolating yourself. I will have to live with this quandary for a while. I won't demand that you show me anything. Perhaps the time will be right later on. I want you to keep a daily diary of all things PowZak.

"Actually, it really is going to come down to one of two things. One, me helping you cope with your new discovery, an incredible drug that will definitely change the world as we know it. Or two, I must treat you as a person who has lost his bearing. Either way, we have work to do."

Chapter Ten

"He wants me to call him Antonio. Actually...Shit, now he has me saying it. Actually, I rather like the guy. He's no dummy. He wants me to keep a daily diary, as if I don't have enough to do."

"How often are you going to see him?"

"Twice a week."

"Do you think that's enough?"

"No, Daphne, I think we should put him up in our guest room, and I could see him three times a day, for Christ's sake."

"All I asked is do you think that's enough. There is no need for hostility. I am not your enemy."

"Sorry, Daphne." Zachary grabs his wife in a vise grip, lifts her off the ground, and cradling her, walks over to the couch and sits her on his lap. "You know, we haven't been close since the fucking FBI raided our house. Are we going to let them scare us?"

"Not a chance, but this isn't a good time. I have my period."

"I don't care. We can just lie close to each other. I'd rather spend ten minutes talking to you than make love to all the cuties in the Victoria's Secret catalog."

Daphne was wondering if he would feel sexy after what had happened. She had convinced herself that there was no way he would want sexual closeness, since she had essentially forced him to see a shrink. She was nearly one hundred percent sure that they would return to their previous state of non-contact. After all, she's empathetic, how could she be wrong? She was wrong.

After watching a BBC production of Sherlock Holmes, Daphne was close to falling asleep.

"Don't wait up for me. I'm going to my study and jot down some ideas I have about work."

Daphne was going to ask him which work, IBX or PowZak, but she held it in.

This is getting complicated, Zachary thinks as he turns on his Italian floor lamp. He knows Daphne doesn't have her period, because it almost always comes at the beginning of the month. It's now the tenth. He wonders if she's pregnant. *Perhaps she's afraid to trust me because she thinks I'm delusional.*

»«»«»«‹›»»»

"This is my first day back at work, so everybody wish me luck." The Warren family had managed to get themselves to the breakfast table without Zachary hitting his crash cymbal.

"You'll do fine. Just don't take any shit from overpaid CEOs or lobbyists," Emma says as she kisses his cheek.

"Language, Em." Daphne tries to hide a smile at her daughter's comment. "What are they teaching you at school, to curse like a sailor?"

"They're trying to program me into being a teenage consumer who will subjugate herself to the American corporation and pay no attention to women's rights or to the environment. Is that what you want me to do, or can I be myself?"

"God, Em, you're so dramatic! I want you to conform. If all the girls are wearing garbage bags on their heads, you are to wear a garbage bag. If the girls are mixing anchovies with their ice cream, you are to do the same. Is that clear?" Zachary says. "I don't want another free-thinking, radical,

129

know-it-all feminist in this house. One is bad enough. You are to be a zombie." He gives Emma a big hug.

Zachary has bought a small computer with ten-inch screen. He keeps it in the accessory compartment of his briefcase. This is where he will keep his PowZak diary for Dr. Principo. After the FBI raid, he dare not keep sensitive material on his home computer. He backs everything up and hides the disks in his classical CD jewel cases.

After a busy morning orienting himself to his new job and office, he unpacks his lunch kit. Every day, no matter how busy she is or how much she has to do, Daphne always fixes him a world-class lunch. He welcomes the extra time it gives him alone. He doesn't like the cafeteria food and eats out only when it's part of a business meeting. Today he has a hot thermos of homemade chili, a cold thermos of homemade Greek yogurt dessert, and Irish soda bread with sweet butter. He's the only executive who eats lunch in his office. He takes out his new computer and opens the Windows 7 Word File.

He types: Dear Diary...*No, I hate that. It's so cliché. I know, I'll simply list the date.*

November 11. Last night, when I tried to be close to Daphne, she lied to me about having her period. I was upset because I didn't know the reason. Perhaps I could have been wrong, but I saw none of the usual indicators that it was her time. I was wondering if she was pregnant. I couldn't suggest that she use a drugstore testing kit, because that would have been a direct implication that I didn't believe her. So, I decided to find out for myself. I went into my study and took a teaspoonful of PowZak and an electrical stimulation of 110 watts DC at three milliamps.

Daphne thought I was in my study. I tiptoed down the hall and turned myself into a flea, right outside our bedroom door. Let me tell you, those little suckers can jump. I could easily leap over two hundred times my body height. So I hopped across the floor completely undetected and crawled onto Daphne's side of the bed.

I hopped on top of her and crawled inside her nightgown. I changed myself into a sperm and went for a swim. Let me tell you, those little suckers can move at a very high rate of speed, but they still take three to five days to reach the egg. I turned myself into a super-sperm. Think of me as a Mini-Cooper with a Ferrari engine. I was moving my tail back and forth at hyper-speed. It was neat being in there, sort of reminded me of the warm salt-water swimming pool when we vacationed in Florida. The Fallopian tubes, those amazing oviducts, reminded me of the Lincoln Tunnel in New York City.

When I got to the end of the tunnel, I looked around for the egg. There it was: no, not pregnant. I must admit, for a brief second I almost jumped in. But that would have put me out of action for nine months until I could reappear as a tiny version of myself. Then what would I do, morph back into the adult me after being missing for all that time? How would I then explain where the baby disappeared? Not all impulses should be acted upon.

I digress. Well, I high-tailed it out of there, and let me tell you, I feel sorry for all babies. Do you know what a shock it was to leave that warm, moist, lovely environment and jump back into a sixty-two-degree room? I landed on the cold sheet and tumbled to the floor. I gathered myself, hopped back down the hall, into my study, and changed back into my human form. I used a tissue saturated with compound A antidote to wipe down the spoon. I no longer need to swallow the PowZak with a glass of water. No, Daphne is not pregnant. I sort of wish she were.

What a miracle life is. How can a couple casually choose to have an abortion? I can understand it for medical reasons, or as a solution for rape victims, but not for convenience.

I find it neat that I can morph into lower life forms. I remember an old black and white movie about the incredible shrinking man. He kept getting smaller and smaller. At one stage, he grabbed a straight pin, the kind you use in sewing. He was so small it became his sword. He used it to kill a spider that was after him. At the end of the movie, he was so tiny he crawled through the grid of a screen. Each grid was as large as he was tall, so the poor chap was shrinking fast. Who knows, perhaps he ended up as a protozoa.

They say that bacteria will inherit the Earth. Theoretically, I can produce intelligent bacteria that will have a knowledge of their own existence. The neat thing about that is their cities will be rather small, and no one will be driving a Ford Explorer. By the time they re-evolve into higher life forms, they would be some smart and capable entities.

But since they would have human roots, namely mine, they would probably just start another uncivilized cycle of desperate creatures who again devolve to their own demise. I guess that's my quandary.

So, Doc, I ask myself what I'm ultimately going to do with this drug. What do I hope to accomplish? That really is an infantile question considering what I've been through, and ignores the basic fact that we have an untested formula with unknown capabilities. I've decided to experiment awhile longer, then perhaps I should destroy it. I guess it all boils down to my opinion of the human race. If I gave everything to Cornell University, would PowZak be used for good or evil? Is man capable of higher evolution? It gives me a fucking headache.

«««‹›»»»

November 12 and 13. It's good to be back at the IBX lab. I love that Titan microscope. I thought about setting up a lab of my own, but it's just too expensive, and we really don't have the space. I had an important breakthrough in testing and development. Actually, it was a milestone. Today, the 12th, I succeeded in creating a binary split. I was able to take a single cell, one that had been treated with PowZak, and

133

while it was growing, I introduced an opposing "magnetic" force. Think of it as a magnet that's able to react to human tissue. It's really not an electrical magnet, but the bio-chemical action is highly involved and would take a hundred pages to explain.

The cell split in two, but retained all its growth cycle. It became two distinct cells of the exact same size. This was a perfect cloning. Some scientists would call it an un-spontaneous regeneration.

The next day I was able to alter either cell after it had split. What does all this mean in real terms? Theoretically, I can give PowZak to a host, have the host morph into any creature, and this is most important, while it is still morphed into the creature, it can spin itself off into another entirely different entity without altering itself. You would then have two distinctly separate and different changlings that originated from the same root. The process will be controlled by the original host.

Again, and this is just a theory, it may be possible for that second changling to create a third, and the third a fourth, and so on. The implications are mind-boggling. Doc, think of a great artist with an infinite palette. Instead of primary colors and cobalt blue, alizarin crimson, that sort of thing, he has a universal prism. He dips his brush into the "paint" on his palette and reproduces exactly what is in his mind in every known color and shade.

Theoretically I could create a squadron of men who are twenty feet tall, can jump three hundred feet into the air, run at four hundred miles per hour, lift fifty tons over their heads, have skin as hard as high-tensile steel and the brain power of a thousand Pentium computers. Now you can see why I don't want the U.S. government to get its hands on PowZak. They would probably all become Republicans.

November 14. I know I'm seeing you tonight, but I wanted to record the first tests of my binary-split, cloning theory. I decided to do the whole thing in my study before I left for work. My household is slow to wake, and I knew I wouldn't be disturbed. I locked the door and took some PowZak. I again turned myself into a flea. I then was able to clone myself into another flea. Then I was able to clone that second flea into a third. So there we sat, on the rug, me, myself, and I, side by side by side. But this isn't exactly what I described to you earlier. I spoke of a different morphing. I had the third flea create a carpet beetle. I had the carpet beetle create a sow bug. So now there were five of us: three fleas, a carpet beetle, and a sow bug. We did some neat formations. First we marched in a straight line, then did figure eights, then we climbed up the base of the floor lamp.

The most interesting part of this experiment is that I could merge the feelings of each creature. I was aware of my ability to jump (the flea), my insatiable appetite for nasty things (the carpet beetle) and my desire to find a soggy piece of wood and roll up into a ball (the sow bug). This experiment was a complete success. The next step is for me to morph into multiple higher life forms.

«‹«‹‹‹›››»›

"Mom, I'm going to see Dr. Principo every so often, weekly if necessary. He promised he would advise me if he thought Zachary needed any medication or further treatment in a controlled environment. He won't tell me any more than that because, as you know, there is a strict rule about doctor-patient privacy."

"What are you going to do if they have to send him away? I hate to be so blunt, Daphne, but we must look at reality. I'm concerned about you and the children."

"So am I, but you know, it's really strange. He is perfectly fine in every other way. He's completely rational and well-balanced in his daily life, with the kids, on the job. He's sexy, funny, and full of life."

"Maybe he appears so, but don't forget outward appearances can easily mask internal torment. You never know if there's a volcano inside. Especially with Zak, because he's so smart and complicated."

"That's ridiculous. I'm not afraid of Zachary, and don't let him hear you call him Zak. I'm afraid *for* Zachary but not *of* him. Still, I don't entirely trust him because of the outrageous comments he has made. Right after he read that Edward Randall story about PowZak, he went off the deep

136

end. I'm frightened because I really don't know what will happen to him or to us. He's always been faithful to me and I to him. I'll stick by him, but lack of trust is getting in the way."

"But he's such a moody bastard."

"Do you know something, Mom, I have never heard you say anything complimentary about my husband. You have a quick, negative trigger-finger, but can never find anything of value in him. Why is that?"

"Because he makes my daughter unhappy, that's why."

"Let me tell you something, Mom: the human body heals itself. A happy person with a happy mind will also heal himself. Look at the Sidtherns, who you recommended to us. Do you realize that they are a complete mess? They gave us a horrible sex video that they should have been watching themselves. You're a marriage counselor, so you feel that everybody should go into counseling the minute they hit a rough spot. Do you know that they record their patients' conversations in the waiting room? Zachary discovered it, and I have no idea how he did it, but somehow he was able to detect the camera. We made up a dialogue about bringing home obese ballet dancers and bisexuals; I don't remember exactly what we said. We also mentioned vacationing with the Sidtherns to film new sex videos. I can't wait to see how they react to that. What a joke. They should be reported."

"I'm counseling them, and as you know, I can't divulge anything that's been said. All I will say is that things are not as they seem. They are good people, and you should continue your therapy."

"Does one therapist *ever* say something bad about another therapist? Sounds like a little self-protection here. Don't forget, I'm also a member of this fraternity. I have no patience with charlatans. Got to go, Mom. Time to take Em to soccer practice."

《《《〈〉》》》

Zachary left IBX at 3:00 to go to the Aesculapius Medical Center in South Burlington. It was time for his yearly physical. He is actually about six months overdue. He was informed by mail that has a new doctor, since his old one moved to North Carolina.

"Dr. Warren, pleased to meet you. My name is Joshua Feldman, and I started here three months ago. I'm very interested in your work at IBX. Can you tell me anything about your new drug? Perhaps we can have lunch if you are pressed for time now."

"Pleased to meet you, Josh. Just call me Zachary, but never Zak, and I would love to show you what we've done. You're welcome to visit IBX any time."

"Pleased to meet you as well, Zachary, never Zak, and I'm Joshua, never Josh." The two men share a hearty laugh.

138

"Do you have any complaints, anything hurting, that sort of thing? I looked at your past history and your blood tests, and everything seems fine. You are seeing Dr. Principo, I gather. Is there anything you want to put into the record?"

"Nothing, really. As a matter of fact, I'm seeing him this evening. A little adjustment now and then is necessary for the mind to be as healthy as the body."

"You know, Zachary, I think it's the opposite. A healthy mind will usually produce a healthy body. There are a lot of miserable, depressed people out there who are as sick as dogs." The two men laugh again. "So, it says here that you work out regularly. What kind of exercise?"

"I love canoeing, cycling, and I have a home gym in the basement. My daughter Em is always catching me doing ab crunches, rowing, and using the Nautilus weight bench. She says I'm obsessed with my abs." *I wonder if Dr. Goldman will notice the large segmented ridge above my navel.*

"Yup, you're fit, all right. I don't believe I've ever seen a man, or a woman either for that matter, who had firmer muscle tone in this area." Zachary is lying on his back on the exam table, and the doctor presses hard into his abdomen with the palm of his hand. "I believe you would stop a .22. What do you eat, Kevlar sandwiches?"

Chapter Eleven

"Dr. Principo, what can you do for Zachary? I'm so upset, I can hardly get through my day. If it weren't for the kids, I'd probably fall apart completely."

"It's important for you to take time for yourself, enjoy the good parts of your life. You are not in control of the outcome. None of us really is. I assure you I will do my best. Zachary is functioning well in all areas."

"Is he delusional?"

"I don't know. It's much too early to say."

"For God's sake, Doctor, he thinks he's a horsefly and a seagull!" Daphne raises her voice. "I may not have your eminent qualifications, but I do have an MA. I believe I know a delusional person when I see one, especially if I live with that person each and every day. What kind of treatment do you recommend?"

"Daphne, you have a great knowledge of psychology and of your husband, but you are too close to render an accurate judgment. This is a time for me to work on understanding the nature and depth of his illness, if there is one. Then I will proceed with treatment."

"Assuming he is delusional, what kind of treatment will you recommend?"

"I will treat this as a hypothetical question, since right now you and I cannot assume anything. Delusional disorder is difficult to treat for many reasons. Foremost is the patient's denial that there's anything wrong. First, I must establish empathy. Second, and this is where you come in, I must educate the family and make them a part of the decision-making process. Direct confrontation of the delusional symptoms is unwise and usually counterproductive. I believe in using medication judiciously, for instance, to control anger or severe depression."

"Do you think he will have to be hospitalized?"

"Only if there is a potential for violence, if he shows signs of harming himself or others, or if he can no longer function."

"What about Primozide? Studies show a sixty-eight percent full recovery rate, and a twenty-two percent partial recovery rate."

"Yours must be a hypothetical question, since it's too early to say. Somatic delusions are more responsive to antipsychotic therapy than other types of delusions. However, there are differences in response rates for patients with persecutory delusions. Most types of delusion have not been clearly defined, and the treatment outcomes are not generally predictable. It gets complicated."

"Doctor, I guess I'm in over my head."

"Not at all, Daphne. You *must* be a part of the solution. You are on your lunch hour, right?"

"Yes."

"Excellent! Take some nut tarts back with you, but don't let Zachary see them, because he'll know where you've been. I don't want him to feel that he's being stalked. I see him this evening at seven-thirty. Try not to worry. We've started down the road to recovery. All will be well."

»«««◊»»»

November 14th, continued. I just occurred to me that this diary must not be a historical record of my treatment. By all means, read what I've written. If I decide to destroy PowZak, and it may well happen, I do not want a diary left behind documenting and confirming its existence.

"That's fine by me, Zachary. Wow, those are some entries. Just like the Lincoln Tunnel, eh? That's amazing."

"It sure was. Do you know how difficult it is for a sperm to reach the egg? First, there are all sorts of anti-microbial agents that are present in women and act as a natural defense against disease. Only the fastest and strongest sperm gets to complete the journey. You would think, with such a natural selective process, demanding such a high degree of strength and stamina, that all people who were born as a result of this fertilization would be spectacular life forms. Unfortunately, most people are shitheads."

"Must be bad sperm," Dr. Principo says in complete seriousness. "You can have strength and stamina and still not have a brain in your head. Which bug did you most enjoy morphing into?"

"The sow bug. All living creatures, whether they know it or not, have a niche. We all have a place where we are happiest. An alpha male who is a superb athlete is happiest when he's scoring a touchdown. A nurturing female, when she is caring for a baby. A sow bug is happiest when it's curled up inside a warm, moist decaying piece of wood. What's really neat is that by changing into all these different creatures, I retain what it's like to feel and think as they do. That's not totally true, because they don't think. It is me

143

supplying the thoughts after remembering what it was like living like a flea, a seagull, or a sow bug."

"I see, tell me more."

"I can tell you one thing for sure. Wild creatures have more going on upstairs than some of those human shitheads who have been spermed. Dogs and cats can reason. Let me tell you about cats. They never forget anything. When I was in college I had a band. We would rehearse at each other's houses. One day, when it was at my house, the guitar player got terrible feedback on his microphone. My cat, Piccolo, ran out of the room and into the basement. From that day forward, whenever he saw a guitar or an amplifier, he would hide in the basement. And get this, even if there was a guitar on television. He would recognize it and flee to his sanctuary."

"How's work?"

"Fine. Quite frankly, I'm tearing it up."

"How are you and Daphne getting along?"

Zachary pauses for ten seconds to measure his words. "She won't make love to me because she doesn't trust me. I'm paying a high price for honesty about my discovery. I'm not believed. Oh sure, she's friendly and caring, but I see extreme fear and anxiety. I feel like a total failure. What good is it if I make the most important discovery ever known to science, if I hurt the people I love the most?"

"Actually, that's something we discussed earlier. Remember, the religion bit."

"Yes, I do, Dr. Principo. I remember it very well. I want you to know that I am totally aware of the damage I am causing. I am totally aware of the choice between love of family and my duty to continue with the most important research ever done. I am not devoid of feelings."

I've never encountered a patient who was so entrenched in his delusions that he can work out cause and effect. He knows all the byproducts. How am I going to dig this out? I may try hypnosis. Dr. Principo writes in his journal. Zachary can see that his expression is more dour than usual.

"You do not have a poker face, Dr. Principo. I can see that you are troubled by my statement."

"Actually, you are probably right about my lack of a poker face. But I'm not necessarily troubled, just confused. You are a complicated son of a bitch. Here, have a nut tart."

«««‹›»»»

Emma has been asked to play on the varsity soccer squad. The South Burlington High School team barely has a winning record. They need to win the next game to make the playoffs. Unfortunately, they play at Central Valley Union, which has the best team in Vermont. They are undefeated. The Warren family is dressed warmly because the temperature is a chilly forty-two degrees.

145

The situation doesn't look good for Emma's team. The refs are obviously catering to the CVU coach and the home team, because they're ranked number one in the state.

"Whoa! That was a deliberate foul! Yellow card, where's the yellow card!" Daphne is shouting at the official.

"I don't like Em playing on that wet grass," Zachary says. "I know it's clear now, but it rained hard a few hours ago. She can turn an ankle very easily. They constantly dry off the ball, but they can't dry off their sneakers. Even with the special tread, it's dangerous. I told her that the player who fakes first on the wet grass has the advantage, because the other player can't react as fast. If someone fakes her, she's not to react instantly, or she'll slide right down. It's best to anticipate the other player's moves. I told her she has to read the other player's mind."

"Where did you learn so much about soccer? That's good advice. Oh shit, Zachary, they are mobbing Em, she can't get near the ball. They must have had scouts at the SB practice game, and they are keying on her. I guess that's good defense, but there's another illegal check. Ref, you must be totally blind! Call the game right, you moron!"

"You're a dildo," Ethan shouts.

Zachary is amused at Daphne's reaction. Now he knows why she was captain of her Nordic ski team. Talk about a soccer mom. The score is CMU 2 and SB 0. The first period is over and Em's team looks really tired.

He remembers his successful experiment that resulted in being able to clone himself into two fleas, a carpet beetle, and a sow bug. He also knows that since his drug is a combination of all substances, namely animal, vegetable, mineral, and electrical energy, he can morph into inanimate objects, if he so chooses.

"Daphne, I'll be right back. Do you want a hotdog?"

"No thanks."

Zachary always carries his atomizer with him. He walks behind the bleachers and squirts fifty short blasts of PowZak into his mouth. "Must be a heavy date, mister." He hadn't seen a CVU cheerleader, who is watching him. Both Zachary and Daphne have star-quality good looks and instantly attract attention wherever they go.

"Even heavier than that. I'm trying to impress my wife, and she's seen it all." The cheerleader giggles and walks away shaking her pompoms.

Zachary notices that they are shuttling in a new dry ball at every stoppage of play. While sitting next to Daphne, he morphs into a soccer ball and places himself on the rack next to the other balls. He is completely dry and is ready to go into the game. He also retains his human shape as he sits in the bleachers.

"Who are you? I thought I knew all the soccer balls at CMU." The ball next to him is speaking.

"My name is Zachary. What's yours?"

"Wilson. That's what it says; just read it."

"No need to get hostile, Wilson. I was just trying to be friendly."

"Friendly, huh. How would you like to be kicked by twenty-two people back and forth across a wet grass field for ninety minutes? And what about my cousin, Nike? They bounce him on a hardwood floor over and over again. He gets passed back and forth among ten sweaty people who then slam him through a net that gives him rope burns.

"My other cousin, Rawlings, was hit by a wooden bat and driven into a metal pole four hundred feet away. The perpetrator wasn't even charged. The creep makes millions of dollars a year for the deed. Thousands of people cheered when Rawlings hit his head on that pole. It's the same here. You get booted by some manic female and everyone cheers. Fans who attend sporting events are obviously sadists.

"For your information, Zachary, our people have been persecuted all over the world by every nationality and with

148

every conceivable indignity. We have been hit through wickets. What the hell is a wicket, anyway? We have been thrown and slung against concrete walls. My attractive sister, Adidas had the yellow fuzz knocked off her private parts by some kind of carbon-fiber racket in the hands of a sadistic, temperamental, Spanish tennis player.

"My big heavy cousin, Brunswick, thought he would be safe from being thrown in the air or kicked around a grass field like we are, but he was wrong. They drilled three holes in him and launched him down a slick wooden lane into ten hard bowling pins. He then had to tumble in the dark, down a gutter that sent him back for more punishment.

"If you are thinking about that other game that doesn't use a round ball, you'd better think again. My Grandfather Sam Spalding started out round, but because he had been squished by huge linemen, and kicked over fifty yards through goal posts, he had become misshapen. All his offspring have been genetically compromised. The poor man was kicked so hard he has stitches on his outside. They grab the stitches to throw him, but never once do they ask him if he's in pain.

"Zachary, it's time for us to get even. On December 7th, another day that will live in infamy, we are going to have World Deflation and Unraveling Day. My brothers, sisters, cousins, and I are all going to go flat at the same time. In the past, no matter how hard we were hit, no matter how severe the mistreatment, we were always expected to bounce back.

Not on December 7th. When we are kicked, thrown half-court, or hit with a racket, we will go flat and not reach the basket or the net. When we are hit with a bat, we will unravel with our stitches, leather, and inner cores flying in all directions.

"Then where will these sadists be? There will be no more *Sports Illustrated Magazine*. They'll have to run fifty-two swimsuit issues. There will be no more tennis, baseball, football, basketball, soccer, lacrosse, racketball, cricket, or any other game insulting to our people. Finally we will be avenged. Are you with us, Zachary? Did I ever tell you about my second cousin, Puck?

"Hell, yeah! I'm with you," he shouts as he is grabbed and switched for a wet ball.

Zachary gets headed by a heavy CVU forward. *Dyed blonde,* he thinks as he is headed toward the sidelines and out of bounds. Some of her color rubbed off next to his center seam. *Ow! I see what Wilson means.*

"Zachary, Em has a breakaway. Go, Em! Go Em!" She is pounding on her husband's shoulder and stamping her feet on the wooden bench seat. Em kicks the ball, but it doesn't travel in a straight line. It does a zigzag and flies into the net to the right of the goalie. "SCORE!" The Warren family shouts in unison. "Did you see that shot? How did she do that?"

"Must be the wet grass."

《《《《〈〉》》》》

"My Z8's top speed is electronically limited to 155. I removed the chip and can now hit 186. Big deal. There are other cars that are much faster. I bought this back in 2002, the last year BMW made the damn thing. It cost me $128,000. I should have bought a Porsche. I could have gotten a custom turbo for $110,000 and it tops out at 205. The Z8 only gets 14 miles per gallon around town. It cost me an absolute fortune to replace the clutch. Plus, I feel cramped when I drive. Lucky I only use it for short trips. And it's terrible in the snow, downright dangerous."

"Are you saying you want to sell the car? Zachary, are you having environmental pangs of conscience?" Daphne is incredulous.

"I am. I can still get over sixty grand for the damn thing. I will limit myself to another vehicle for that amount or less. I want one that is not so conspicuous. Why did I buy it in red? I can feel the hatred of other motorists when I have the top down. 'Oh look at the rich bastard with his toy.' Perhaps I'll buy a classic car, an old triumph or MG."

"You will still get stares from people who are envious of a young, good-looking man having a good time. You should please yourself. I *do* like the idea of better gas mileage. The first playoff game is Friday afternoon. You are going to be there."

"And if I said no?"

Daphne flashes a wry smile that when translated meant "miss this game and you will feel great pain."

On Friday, the CVU game went into overtime and was won by SB on penalty kicks. A shy girl who scored only one goal all year got the winner. Em scored the other two goals.

"Do you know what Em said yesterday? She said that if she stays healthy, she can win an athletic scholarship to the college of her choice. She said it's neat that we can afford any school she wants, and she is grateful. But if she does it herself, it will be really awesome. This is a fourteen-year-old talking. Do you know what this means? So far, we've done a pretty good job. Put her there, pal."

Zachary vigorously shakes Daphne's hand. He kisses her, but she's withholding and tentative.

"I bought a Volkswagen Eos. It will do 148, has front wheel drive for the snow, and gets way better gas mileage than the Z8. It's a spiffy hard-top convertible. It looks like a regular car, and then presto-chango, the hardtop disappears into the trunk and you have a sun car. No more dirty looks. I also chose a nice, cool, almost cobalt-blue color. It's got some neat electronics, complete SatNav, Sirius radio, and six-CD changer. I even put an inverter in the trunk. There's a receptacle in the back. I can plug it in and run any AC appliance off the car battery. That's great in an emergency. It's also got this unique roll bar that activates automatically if the car leans past a certain angle. That's a great idea, because there are no posts to block your vision."

Zachary picked up his new car. *No more eight cylinders; now I have only five. Engines are amazing. Upstroke explosion, downstroke exhaust, three thousand times a minute. I wonder what it feels like to be a piston?*

Chapter Twelve

Zachary is in the basement gym, working out on his Nautilus Olympic Weight Bench, when he hears a racket in the backyard. He looks out one of the small ground-level windows and sees Emma running around shouting, "No! No!" and he hears a dog yelping. He runs up the stairs and she's standing next to Daphne, who has both hands over her mouth.

"Dad, I tried to stop him. A police dog like the one that visited us was in our backyard and went after a porcupine." Emma points toward the Warren's tree boundary line. Zachary sees an immature porcupine, about fourteen inches long, slowly walking between the rows of his neighbor's woodpile.

"Zachary, he got a face full of these." Daphne bends down and picks up some stray quills. "It isn't right for people to let their dogs roam free. There's a fence-leash law in Shelburne.

Now that poor dog will have to go to the vet to have the quills removed. I wonder who owns him."

"I agree completely. Em, good for you to try to stop him, but it could have been dangerous. That's a very big dog, and he could have turned on you."

"No, he's friendly, I could tell. But I'll bet he won't chase animals for a while.   Mom, Dad, do you know how porcupines make love?"

"How, Em?" Daphne says as she rolls her eyes.

"Very carefully." Emma giggles as she walks back into the house.

Zachary continues working out in his home gym. He's using the rowing machine at a good steady rate of speed. When he finishes the workout, he pauses to rest and puts his hands on his legs to catch his breath. He notices some unusual stubble on his right thigh, right under his shorts. He goes into the bathroom and uses his razor to shave the three hairs. It's a tough job requiring much pressure. He cuts them even with the skin-line, and there are now three noticeable black dots where the hairs were. He takes the hairs back to his study and measures them with a small micrometer.

This is weird. They measure 3.175 millimeters. That's .125 inches. Zachary turns on his computer and does some medical research. He learns that the width of a human hair varies from 40 to 110 microns. For reference, a single sheet of paper is approximately 100 microns or .004 inches. So a human hair is .001 inches. His hairs are over 100 times larger.

First, he noticed his hard, segmented stomach, now he has huge hairs as hard as bone. He suspects there will be additional side effects from PowZak. He's getting much stronger, even without the drug.

«««‹›»»»

Dr. Principo reviews his notes prior to Daphne Warren's visit. For every tangible, positive sign that Zachary fits certain criteria, there is an equal and opposite counterpoint. There wasn't even a term for his supposed disease until 1977 when the term Delusional Disorder was coined. All the signs point to the Grandiose type. The patient honestly believes he's made an important discovery. But this is a rare form. Delusional patients are less than 0.03% of the population and Grandiose patients even fewer. The absence of mania makes it even more uncommon. Grandiose delusional patients are usually narcissistic and show a complete lack of empathy. They are exploitive and possess a high degree of entitlement. Zachary has none of these traits, none! He's kind, generous, and loving toward his family.

There has to be a causative agent, damn it! I suspect trauma of some kind, but oy, what kind, how, when? I will further explore his early childhood. Perhaps his relationship with his aunt isn't as benign as he claims. He will probably be totally resistant to any probing, so I've got to come in the back door. This is going to take some digging. If I fail, there are only two alternatives: hypnosis or drug therapy. But I doubt if he will permit it, and there's no guarantee it will unlock his secrets. I don't have a good report for Daphne, but I must stress that we're just beginning.

«««‹›»»»

"Doctor, I am an empath. In the traditional sense, I am an empathic person with the gift to feel what others are feeling. But whatever is happening to Zachary, there are things I can't explain."

"Daphne, please give me an example."

"As you know, I believe he is delusional to a high degree, yet there are unexplainable physical manifestations. Some are subtle, and some are glaring. For instance, I saw him working out in his home gym. This is not necessarily a big deal; he always does. But I saw the free-weights that he put back on the Nautilus bench. I added up the total weight on both sides of the bar, and it came to 650 pounds. Isn't that impossible for anyone to lift? How can he press 650 pounds, not including the bar?"

"Are you sure he was lifting the entire amount? That is highly unlikely. I know he is strong, but that would be very uncommon."

"Yes, Doctor. Unlikely, uncommon, those are good words. There's more. Let me do a test with you, if you don't mind."

"Absolutely, I'll be happy to oblige."

Daphne takes a sheet of paper and tapes it to the wall. She asks the doctor for a rubber band and shoots it at the paper from a distance of five feet.

"As you can see, Doctor, from this distance, it is virtually impossible to catch this rubber band before it hits the paper. I'm going to sit in a chair right up against this wall and put my hand on my knee. That's roughly the height at which a hand would rest on a table. You shoot this rubber band into the paper, and I'll try to catch it."

Dr. Principo lets the rubber band fly, and it thwacks against the paper before Daphne can react.

"Em was playing with her ballpoint pen. She brought some class notes to the dinner table, and she took the pen apart for some reason. The spring that holds the cartridge popped loose at a speed similar to that rubber band you shot. Zachary was sitting right next to Em, less than two feet away, and he caught the spring out of mid-air and handed it back to her. I didn't even see his hand move. His speed can only be measured in milliseconds. His reaction time is faster than a fucking mongoose. Please try this paper test with him.

"There was another incident. We have replaced all our incandescent light bulbs with the new type, whatever they are called. When we walked into the bedroom, just before he flipped the light switch, he turned to me and said, 'The bulb's going to burn out. It's going to die.' Sure enough, he flipped the switch, and the light flashed brightly and burned out. How did he know that was going to happen? The damned thing was supposed to last for years. See what I mean?"

"Actually, I do see what you mean. I'm troubled because he defies categorization. I'm consulting with my colleagues. We must not jump to conclusions or make any treatment judgments based on our scant evidence. It has been my experience that a nugget will be found. It's hiding somewhere in his past, in some dark recess, but it will out. It is extremely valuable for you to tell me all this.

"Actually, he is a remarkable son of a bitch. Are the two of you getting it on, or perhaps you don't fully trust him?"

Daphne doesn't answer at first but looks down at the floor. "I'm afraid to. The last time we made love I was very frightened. He has a strange power I can't explain. I lose all control and feel like I'm going to be swallowed whole in some primordial ecstasy. I don't want to scare the children."

"It sure beats faking it. Why don't you experiment? It will be good for both of you. Here, have a nut tart."

«««‹›»»»

December 7th. I wonder how Wilson and his family made out in World Unraveling Day. As far as I know, all football

159

and basketball games went on as planned. The specifics of this event would take too much time to write down, so I'll give you the details, Doc, when we meet tomorrow. Daphne and I have been seeing a married couple who are licensed, but horrible, marriage counselors. They openly fight with each other while they are supposed to be helping us. She talked me into seeing them again next week. It's more comic relief for me than anything else, and a total waste of money. They do something extremely illegal that I noticed the last time we were in the waiting room. They hide a video camera in the ceiling and record everything their patients say.

This gave me an idea. A hidden tape recorder or camera is an excellent way to intrude or spy on anyone. As you know, I have the ability to morph into mineral or vegetable objects as well as living beings. I was wondering how I could use this ability to hide somewhere, undetected, and spy on people. I wasn't thinking of anything kinky here, such as turning myself into a coin and hiding in my neighbor's bedroom. No, I wanted to get some hard information, some real dirt.

Did you read about that Tea Party freshman congressman, Alfred Hemming? He's been making a lot of noise criticizing every social program that the president tries to put through. There is a constant litany of anti-common-man, anti-ninety-nine-percent reactionary garbage spewing from his mouth. I thought a man like this has got to have a black heart, and is probably hiding shady and awful secrets.

This is what I did. As I already said, I can morph into anything. I chose a red-tailed hawk because they are great at high altitude cruising. I flew at mach four and directly onto the U.S. Capitol building. It was easy to find Hemming's office. I changed into a fly, flew into his inner office, and then changed into a paperclip tucked neatly under the corner of a stack of papers. I don't know if you are aware of this fact, but most senators and congressman have security personnel who are part of the Capitol Police Force that hunts for bugs and listening devices. If I had tried to smuggle in and plant a bug or digital recorder, it would have quickly been discovered and removed.

There was no one else in the room. I was biding my time when the phone rang. I could easily hear both sides of the conversation. I left nothing to chance. I had a miniature digital recorder built into the clip. It wouldn't be noticed, because it was no larger than flea dirt, and it was way too small to be picked up by a scanner. This is the conversation I recorded while in his office.

"Mark, I agree with you. The protesters need a bath. They are vermin who need to be stopped. In my state we've decided to tear down their tents and use pepper spray. As far as I'm concerned, they have no legal right to assemble. I called the mayors of Atlanta, Boston, Oakland, Miami, and six other cities. We have a plan in place to coordinate the dismantling of these vermin encampments."

"That's real good, Al. I've contacted the FBI, and we've got some great PR people on board who worked for the U.S. Chamber of Commerce. We're going to discredit the protestors and equate their actions with anti-Americanism. They are going to be cast as enemies of the people who are threatening our way of life. I'm getting pressure from some important Wall Street CEOs, and they want to see immediate action. I want you to gather your peers and present a united front in opposition to the so-called ninety-nine-percent rebellion."

"You can count on me, Mark. If this movement gets out of hand, it could influence the American Sheeple. We can't have that, no siree, we just can't have that."

I got what I came for, reversed the morph, clip into fly, fly into hawk, and flew back to my deck. I changed back into myself and went directly to my computer. You know the rest, because you no doubt read it in *The New York Times* a few days ago. I sent the recording and the transcript to the *Huffington Post*, using a different name. They were able to confirm a communication from a Wall Street CEO that was leaked by a disgruntled personal secretary. It matched the information I presented, so they ran the recording and transcript on their website. *The Times* picked it up, and it has also gone viral. Hemmings has so far sloughed it off, claiming it's a fake, but he's stirred up a hornet's nest. The Democrats are making political hay. This could cost the Republicans important votes in the next election. I feel great that I had the idea. PowZak is now a friend of the people. I feel like Robin Hood or John of Arc.

《《《《〈〉》》》》

"Thanks, Mom. Ethan, you be good and help your grandma make ravioli. We'll see you tonight for dinner. I'll bring the salad and dessert." Daphne drops off her son and races back to her home on Bay Road. Emma is at soccer practice, and Zachary had told her he would be home early. He is no longer obsessed with work. He used to be the first one in and the last to leave, but lately he's much more relaxed. They love him at IBX and there's talk of promoting him to a company-wide position, overseeing the entire research and development program, not just for IBX Vermont.

Daphne is predatory. She intends to ambush her husband as soon as he steps into the house. *I'm not afraid of him. I can give as well as get.* She prepares herself for battle, not for lovemaking. *I have all the power here. He can't resist my white satin nightgown. He won't get as far as the hall.* Zachary comes home at the exact time he said. He doesn't have time to shut the front door before Daphne grabs him and they fall down in the entryway.

"Yes, ma'am. I do see that you're all right. Sorry to intrude, ma'am. A passerby heard what she thought was, er, what she thought was a crime in progress. We had to check it out. Have a nice evening."

163

Daphne shrieks with delight. "Oh my God, I hope the Shelburne police don't gossip. Zachary, you are wonderful, do you know that?"

"You are also halfway decent." Zachary grabs Daphne and throws her down on the living room couch.

Afterward, they are resting in each other's arms. Zachary has his feet on the coffee table, and Daphne has one leg on top of his. "Brrr, it's cold in here. Did you shut the front door? God, even your back is hard. How the hell does a person do a back crunch? There is only one soft spot on your whole body, Zak, and it's your head." She baits him, but he just smiles.

"You win, Daffy," Zachary says. "I'm finally too tired."

"You'd better stay awake. Em will be home in a few minutes, and we're eating at Mom's tonight."

"Oh goody!" Zachary says in mock delight.

"Be nice. After all, you should be very happy right now."

"Oh, I am, but not about having dinner at their house. They're so old fashioned about everything. Em is aware that she must read from a script. She can't be herself or she'll make them uncomfortable. If we wear our jeans, they feel slighted. I have to dress fancier for their dinners than I do for my job. We're going to dinner at your parent's house, for Christ's sake, not the White House. They don't have a television in the living room, so the kids run into the basement to play pool. Your dad follows them downstairs to make sure the cat doesn't jump on the table. Oh fun, fun, fun."

"Zachary, it's been six months since we were last over there for a meal. No, I'm wrong, that was just for coffee and cake. It's been almost ten months. Guess what kind of dessert I'm bringing. I made some Italian nut tarts. Dr. Principo gave me the recipe. When you see him Thursday, tell him thanks a million. They are delicious. As a matter of fact, I added a secret ingredient that makes mine better. I want you to take him some and see if he can guess what it is. See if you can guess what it is."

"Mm, I don't know. That *is* tasty. Is it some kind of liqueur? Daphne, that was a splendid idea. You know, we're speaking of him as a friend, not a therapist. He is one skillful son of a bitch. I actually look forward to our sessions."

Zachary is in the bathroom. He uses an electric razor to remove his six o'clock shadow. He has very dark hair, and when they go out, he always has to shave again. He remembers Daphne's comments about his hard back. He takes her hand-held mirror and turns away from the surrounding glass mirror above their double marble sink. He uses the magnifying side to study his back, as the image is reflected in the large mirror. There are small white globe lights top and bottom so the illumination is excellent. He notices mica-like scales, about two inches long and one inch wide on either side of his spinal column, about two inches below his shoulder blades. They must be what Daphne touched when she said his back was so hard.

When he examines them closely, they have a tortoiseshell appearance and are attached only at the top. They are roughly in the same position that wings would be, if he were sprouting them.

Chapter Thirteen

"Hellooo, Zachary, hellooo Daphne, it's been a while since we've seen you guys. I guess it's one month to the day. What's new and exciting?"

Florence Sidthern gives the Warrens her usual bubbly intro, and walks them into the therapy room. Zachary noticed that the camera was gone from the corner of the waiting room ceiling.

Mitchell is sitting at his usual place, holding his usual clipboard, and instead of his fountain pen, he has a gaudy red, white, and blue felt-tip. He doesn't make eye contact with either of them, but looks up quickly and nods hello.

"What happened to your camera?" Zachary asks.

"Oh that," Florence answers. "We decided to move it because we didn't want anyone to get the wrong impression.

I like what you said about me being a hot little number. That's a great idea about making sex videos in Santa Lucia. When do we leave?"

"Very funny, Florence," Mitchell says with mild annoyance. "You know they were baiting us. It was unkind to speak of sexual matters involving your therapists when you assumed we were having difficulty in that area."

"It would be even more unkind if I went to the medical malpractice board and told them about your fucking camera," Zachary says heatedly.

"Any way that a couple can stimulate themselves without hurting anyone is fine with me, and it should be fine with the medical authorities, as well." Mitchell says matter-of-factly. "We would tell them that it was a security system, and it wouldn't raise an eyebrow."

"What? Are you saying that you and Florence use the recordings of your patients in the waiting room as a sexual turn-on?" Daphne rises from her beanbag chair and menacingly leans over the front of Mitchell's desk.

"Whatever floats your boat," Florence says as she and Mitchell smile broadly. "Your last visit was wonderful and helped us understand your thought processes."

"You are both kinky bastards," Daphne says. Zachary puts his right hand over his forehead. "How can you be our therapists, our advocates, when you use our dialogue for your own enjoyment? What else do you do, record our therapy sessions and put them on YouTube?"

"You fell for our act, and it brought you closer," Mitchell says. "When a couple in trouble sees another dysfunctional couple, they react in one of two ways. One, they recoil in complete aversion. Or two, they see the other couple's problems and don't want to go down the same road, and it brings them closer. We monitored the two of you in great detail. In your relationship, where there is a lot of heat but some minor block preventing your union, it worked like a charm. Florence and I have never been apart. Nor have we had any sexual dysfunction. You've been had, and you're the better for it. Now let's talk about trust. Daphne, do you trust Zachary? Zachary, do you trust Daphne?"

"I don't trust either of *you*. How much do we owe you for this session? We're out of here," Zachary says as he puts on his navy-blue pea coat and wool hat.

"This is a normal reaction," Florence says. "You will realize that this is the best place to talk about your troubles. Our new, honest relationship and communication will stay in your mind. When or if things get rough again, you know where to find us. Mitchell and I suspected that you were about ready to 'graduate' from the Sidthern Academy. We wish you the best and much love. Don't forget the ylang ylang oil. Let us know when you want to visit Saint Lucia."

On the drive back from their therapists, Daphne was working up a high degree of agitation. "It wasn't an act, and you know it. They don't have degrees in drama, but they do have PHDs in deception. What about Mitchell and his fountain pen? He was so pissed at Florence that he broke the nib, and the ink ran down his pants leg. Sure, some act. They're both full of shit, and I'm going to the malpractice board."

"I agree, Daphne, but I have to confess, I think they are both very funny. I can't wait to tell Dr. Principo about their antics. I wonder what he will suggest? I do believe Florence was half-serious about our taking them to Santa Lucia, wherever the hell that is."

"It's Saint Lucia, and it's a tropical island in the Eastern Caribbean. It was voted the best honeymoon destination eight times by World Travel Awards." Daphne blushes because she knows that she has betrayed herself.

Zachary sits at the traffic light too long. It turns green, but he looks at Daphne as the driver directly behind them honks his horn. "Someone has been doing research on the Internet, hasn't she? What's on your mind, young woman?"

"I thought we might take a vacation there, with the kids, of course. It's a fascinating volcanic island with beautiful beaches. It gets gray and ugly here by the end of February."

"Oh Daffy, I'm disappointed. You mean Mitchell and Florence won't be joining us?"

«««<>»»»

"You have been my friend and colleague for thirty years. Of course I respect your opinion." Dr. Principo has seen Zachary, and he is conferring by telephone with a specialist in delusional disorder and schizophrenia. "With this patient, I break all the rules. He's so smart that he will detect any repeat patterns or attempts at manipulation. I never sit in the same place. I vary the physical distance between doctor and patient. I walk around the room. I feed him nut tarts. Now he's convinced he's a paperclip with a built-in tape recorder. He morphed into a red-tailed hawk and soared into some congressman's office after changing himself into a fly, and then into a paperclip. He says he recorded this Tea Party slob bad-mouthing the Wall Street protestors. He claims he sent the recordings to the Huffington Post."

"Why should I do that? It's completely irrational. If I call Huffington and ask them that, they will put *me* away. So what if I learn the truth about who sent them the recording? I still can't confront my patient with what I know. He will retreat further into his delusion. I've never seen a case like this one. He has none of the typical accompanying symptoms: no mania, no schizophrenia, no paranoia, no displayed violence of any kind. He is extremely high-functioning in all areas. His wife is an empathic psychologist, and even she can't explain some of the things he does.

"So what do I do, continue to redirect his grandiose delusions, or enter into them as if I believed what he is saying? I've yet to explore his early life in great detail. He's extremely reluctant to talk about his childhood."

"You're probably right, Pierre; there has to be something hidden. This guy looks like a movie star, is as strong as a gorilla, and smarter than the computer he uses. He has everything going for him. He's rich, has great social skills, is a kind person who loves his wife and family, has an important job, and is highly respected. Pierre, it makes no sense that he should be captive in an unreachable delusion. So when are you and Hilda coming to Vermont? We have a guest room waiting.

"No, I don't want you to visit just to see my patient. Stop trying to analyze me! Okay, you're right, but you could have fun anyway. How about before Christmas? I know, Florida is nice and warm. Don't be such a geezer; a little below zero will invigorate you. Hilda used to love cross-country skiing, and you still have family here. What do you mean, you don't speak? Am I talking to a plumber with a leaky faucet? Shame on you, Pierre. That's the main reason you should visit us."

《《《〈〉》》》

December 11th. Doc, I have a lot to write about, so I'll get to it. I decided to visit Saint Lucia in the Eastern Caribbean. The distance from Shelburne, Vermont to Saint Lucia is 2,700 miles. I really like to morph into a red-tailed hawk. It has become my favorite mode of travel. Although I can speed much faster, I enjoy mach four. That's about 3,072 miles per hour, depending on my altitude. Total flying time is a little over fifty minutes from Vermont to the island. Since I'm not metallic, and was flying low over the water, I was hoping I wouldn't trigger any Air Force early warning radar. The last thing I need is to be the cause of scrambling fighter jets to intercept a bird. But of course, they couldn't catch me if they tried.

Saint Lucia is really neat from the air. It's very mountainous. The highest is Mount Gimie at 3,120 feet, but by far the prettiest are the twin peaks of Gros Piton and Petit Piton. You can really see the volcanic origins in these hills. Just for the fun of it, I pretended to be a jet plane and landed at George F. L. Charles Airport on the coast. It's on the outskirts of Castries, the largest city, and wow, is that coastline gorgeous. November is right at the end of their rainy season, and December is supposed to start their dry season, but I flew through a delightful shower on the way in. The air temperature was about eighty-five degrees. There was a double rainbow between the Piton peaks. A hawk's vision is incredible. It's like wearing a permanent pair of fifty-power binoculars. I could see dozens of places unlike anything I have seen in America.

I decided to morph into several life forms. The first was a generic human. I chose a dark-skinned male person (by the way, doc, I'm going to see what it's like to be a female as soon as I can work up my courage) of average height. Saint Lucia's people are mostly African and mixed African-European. Just about everyone speaks English, but ninety-five percent of the population speaks Kweyol, which is a kind of French referred to as Patois. It guess it's similar to what they speak in New Orleans. I studied French in college, and it was easy to learn 10,000 words and perfect the accent. I was going to morph into a Rastafari, but I don't think I could be as convincing. They are in a two percent minority.

Do you know what's really wild? Saint Lucia has the highest ratio of Nobel laureates per capita of any country in the world. Sir Arthur Lewis won for Economics in 1979 and Derek Walcott for Literature in 1992. And, get this, they were both born on January twenty-third, which so happens to be *my* birthday. Is there a coincidence here? This *is* about PowZak. I'm not saying I'm in the same league as those gentlemen. That will be for someone else to judge. If you don't believe me about the Nobel prizes, just look it up in Wikipedia.

By the way, you'll be interested in this: the total population is only 174,000 people, yet they have several medical schools. There's International American University, Destiny University School of Medicine, and Spartan Health Sciences University. The leading secondary school for boys is St. Mary's College. Both Nobel laureates studied there. For an island that's only twenty-seven miles long and fourteen miles wide, that ain't too shabby.

The people of Saint Lucia like to boogie. Every Friday night they have "jump-ups," which are street parties. Locals and tourists mix it up. Oh baby, the food is incredible.

There are barbecued meats, dasheen, seafood cooked over hot coals, and barbecued chicken. Islanders claim that if you drink a sea-moss shake, which is seaweed, milk, sugar, and fruit, you'll keep jumping throughout the night. I tried one but got tired anyway. That's probably because I had three pina coladas at Shamrock's Pub in Rodney Bay.

There's some touristy stuff. I'm not crazy about the steel bands, but there's lively street dancing everywhere that goes on until two in the morning. Actually, they are a *very* musical people. They dance the quadrille, calypso, reggae, compas, salsa, and others. They have an International Jazz Festival. Daphne loves jazz. I can't wait to take her to a jump-up.

I really wanted to see the island, so I morphed into a jacquot. I know you're going to ask me what a jacquot is. I was a seventeen-inch-long parrot. It's the national bird. I was mainly green with a few iridescent patches of blazing red and blue on my wing tips. I had dark red on my chest and light blue on top of my head feathers. Doc, it's impossible to remain obscure with such plumage, but I enjoyed looking at my reflection in puddles. Daphne says I'm vain. She's probably right. Did you know that, like geese, parrots mate for life, which can be up to eighty years. There is absolutely nothing more beautiful than flying at dawn, just above the tree canopy in a tropical rain forest.

You're not going to believe what I found: a drive-in volcano. The smell of sulfur was strong and, as a parrot, I had an increased sensitivity, so I didn't linger very long. But it was wild. It's in Soufriere, and all the tourist handouts boast that it's the only drive-in volcano in the world. It isn't considered active but does have boiling mud pools and steam venting. People live all around the base, so I suppose it's dormant. That's an interesting place to have a home. Only optimists need apply. A lot of people bathe in the sulfur springs. They supposedly have medicinal qualities, especially for people with dermatological problems.

There are numerous hiking trails in the rainforest. There's a park covering about 19,000 acres, and I wanted to check it out. I morphed from the parrot into a mongoose. I figured if there were any poisonous snakes on the island, a mongoose was the creature to be. There are exotic birds everywhere, at least thirty species, and the flowering vines are other-worldly. I did see some humans on the trails. As you know, a mongoose is weasel-like, and can move at a decent rate of speed. I enjoyed walking on the trails, that is, until I met Mr. Fer-de-Lance.

You know, Doc, it seems that every positive experience has an equal and opposite negative. It's like firing a gun. For the bullet to go forward, there's a strong recoil backward. So it was with my walking in the rainforest. Mr. Fer-de-Lance is a very ugly poisonous pit-viper. I was just poking along, enjoying being a mongoose and taking in all the flora and fauna. I went off the trail to study some flowers, and scampered across a water run-off, about four feet deep. That was my big mistake. This ugly snake was at the bottom. I got way too close to it before I knew it was there. I couldn't go forward, because it blocked my way. I couldn't turn around, because I would be vulnerable to the snake's strike. This fucker was about seven feet long. It was copper red in color and had a huge triangular-shaped head. The damned thing lunged at me. I grabbed it behind the head, but it wriggled free and threw me against the bank. I could hear its tongue slithering in and out and could smell the poison from its glands.

It lunged at me again, but I got a really good grip behind his head. I was squeezing my jaw as hard as I could. We were rolling around in a ditch filled with slimy algae. This time I threw him off. He was writhing in pain, and I quickly returned in the direction I came. He was wise not to come after me. Of all the creatures I have morphed into, and all the situations I've been in, that was the worst. As soon as I returned to the trail, I morphed back into a jacquot and flew the hell out of there. When I was a half-mile out to sea, I changed back into the hawk and flew straight home.

«««‹›»»»

"He spent Friday evening and Saturday morning in his study, working on an IBX project. He doesn't do that very often. He came out about 10:30 and made himself some brunch. He used to work all night at least three times a week, so he's changed for the better. Why do you ask, Dr. Principo?"

"I'm afraid his delusions are getting more bizarre. I don't want to worry you, but I am concerned, Daphne."

Daphne sees that the doctor isn't his usual optimistic and reassuring self. She is anxious and frightened. "What do you mean? How can I help?"

"I've been conferring with my colleague, a brilliant analyst who now lives in Florida. He's an expert in this field. He will be visiting us in December, and I want him to meet Zachary. You can be of great help if you can give me any insights into his early childhood. Does he talk much about his relationship with his aunt? Does he mention his early school days, his friends, that sort of thing?"

"I know you wouldn't be asking me this if you had any idea what his history was like. Perhaps you can't wait for the knowledge to appear as the result of the normal therapeutic process."

"Very good, Daphne, that's exactly why I'm asking you. I don't think he is in any immediate danger, at least I hope not, but I may have to speed up certain elements of his therapy. I don't want him to devolve, regress, or worsen. There probably are a dozen similar useless words we could use that really don't tell the story. I hate to be so personal, and get you so deeply involved, but I know you would want me to. Does he show any signs of abnormal behavior? Anything strange worth noting? How are the two of you getting along?"

"Perfect. He's absolutely perfect. The kids love him. Em told me that she's going to marry a man just like her father. Ethan is his shadow; he follows him everywhere. That is, if he can get me out of the way. Zachary even shows the right amount of impatience and unreasonableness. He will raise his voice and pound the table when he reads about the Tea Party. God, except for this, our lives are perfect."

"Let's concentrate on his early life. Please try to remember any details. Don't write them down, because I don't want him to suspect what we're doing. I'll see you just before Pierre, my colleague, arrives in Vermont. Don't do anything yet about the Sidtherns; I'm going to make some inquiries. I suspect that they might have to be defrocked, but I'd like to gather more facts.

"I hate to admit it, but your nut tarts are better than mine. What did you put in them?"

"Lazzaroni Amaretto."

"Not bad for a Nordic woman. Keep the faith."

Daphne relaxes herself and tries to remember any details that could help her husband's therapy. Dr. Principo wouldn't tell her much about Zachary's visit, or any specifics about his delusions. On the way home from seeing the doctor, she picks up the ingredients for a spinach lasagna. She has a new interest in Italian cooking. *Must be the nut tarts.* She unpacks her canvas bags and puts the food away.

On the kitchen floor, under Zachary's chair, she notices a small cocktail umbrella, the kind they use for tropical drinks. It has a small tear at the edge, and one of the toothpick supports is broken. On the umbrella is a drawing of a leprechaun, and it reads: *Shamrock's Pub, Rodney Bay.*

"Em, Ethan, does this belong to either of you?"

"No, Mom."

She pitches it into the garbage can.

Chapter Fourteen

Zachary is restless and having trouble sleeping. He glances at their custom digital alarm clock, and it reads 3:44. After changing position four times, tossing back and forth, he again checks the clock. It now reads 4:25. The same thing happened the night before. He woke up at 2:27 and 3:11. Three out of four times the total numbers added up to 11. As he lies in bed, staring at the faint green glow from the clock's display, he wonders why the number is 11. Could this be coincidence, or is there a mathematical reason?

There are four digits on the clock. He wonders if 11 is a median number. The highest total occurs at 9:59 when the numbers add up to 23. The median of 23 is 11.5. He computes the total for each time period in a twelve-hour cycle. The numbers add up to 5, twenty-seven times. The numbers add up to 8, fifty times, and so on. He figures the total for each minute, from 1:00 to 12:00.

I am correct. The total numbers add up to 11, sixty-four times. The next highest is 12, with a total of sixty-two times. That's why this is happening. If you glance at the clock often enough, 11 will be the total that shows up most.

He finally puts himself to sleep when he extrapolates seconds, days, and weeks into his equation. It's a Mensa way of counting sheep.

"Everybody up!" Ethan holds a copper-bottomed stainless-steel saucepan and is hitting it with a serving ladle as he walks down the hall. "It's 6:45 and we don't want to be late, so let's get crackin'." He is imitating his father.

Daphne pulls the covers over her head. "Hello, little buddy," Zachary says, cotton-mouthed. "Go back to bed, it's Saturday."

«««‹›»»»

I wonder if I should book a vacation package and surprise the family. No, I'd better not. I don't know what Zachary's work schedule is for January. Daphne is on her way to Champlain Valley Travel. She wants information about Saint Lucia. There is a very pleasant senior woman who is dressed like Maggie Smith in one of her Edwardian Era movies. She talks about flight schedules, prices, and advance booking times. She hands Daphne several brochures.

"Did your family see *Pirates of the Caribbean*?"

"Oh yes, we all loved that," Daphne says. "It was quite a romp, and Johnny Depp is so sexy."

"Did you know that you can see the west side of the island by sea from the decks of the brig *Unicorn*, the ship that was used in the movie? There are many places to stay in Rodney Bay." The agent hands her a brochure for the Cap Maison Resort and Spa.

Daphne remembers the broken cocktail umbrella. She thanks the agent, races back home, and looks in the garbage can. "Em, did you empty the recycling?"

Emma answers yes, and Daphne runs outside and lifts up the cover of the blue bin. She piles pizza boxes, newspapers, wine bottles, cardboard, and all manner of paper and plastic on the ground. Finally, at the bottom of the bin, she finds the umbrella. A glass jar landed on top of it and a few more sticks are broken. She reads *Shamrock's Pub, Rodney Bay*.

She takes the umbrella into Zachary's study. He is reading a book about mathematical probability, sitting in his favorite chair by the window. She sits in his desk chair and swivels it around to face him. The sun is reflecting off the snow and casting shadows from the curtains onto his book. He smiles at her. Daphne holds up the umbrella.

"Is this yours?"

"I was wondering what I did with that thing. Where did you find it?"

"It was on the kitchen floor, under your chair, you must have dropped it. Where did you find it?

"Do you really want to know?"

"Sure, why not, try me." Daphne has an edge to her voice and moves the swivel chair with her feet, off the plastic rug protector, close to Zachary's chair.

"Do you know where Rodney Bay is?"

"Yes I do, I just got back from Champlain Valley Travel and got these brochures. Where did you get the umbrella, from another travel agent?

"You know, Daphne, I hate lying to you. Sometimes I do for your own protection, but I don't like it. Let's just say that I found it."

"Found it where, Zachary?"

He pauses for a long time before he answers. "I found it last Friday."

"That tells me *when* you found it, not *where* you found it." She simultaneously has feelings of intense curiosity, fear, and annoyance.

"I found it at Shamrock's Pub in Rodney Bay. I morphed into a red-tailed hawk and visited the island last weekend. I attended a Jump-Up disguised as a native and drank at the pub. I then morphed into a parrot to see the island. After that I morphed into a mongoose to hike in the rainforest. I got into a terrible fight with a fer-de-lance, an ugly poisonous snake. I morphed back into a parrot, flew offshore, morphed back into the hawk, and flew home in time for Saturday morning brunch. I brought the cocktail umbrella back as a souvenir.

"You will love the jump-ups. They have them every Friday night. They serve food and dance until two in the morning. Did you know that there are three medical schools on that island, and the population is only 174,000?"

"Zachary, I don't know where you got this umbrella. The facts you quoted can easily be found on Wikipedia. The rest of your story is the reason why you are seeing Dr. Principo."

"Daphne, when we lie, we postpone the day of reckoning. It becomes a mushroom growing in a dark closet. All evil starts with lies. I've told my share, either by omission or outright falsehoods, to make my life more comfortable. Telling the truth isn't always the easiest way. As a matter of fact, it can be downright terrifying. I don't know what I can do to re-assure you that I'm not two sandwiches short of a picnic."

"Anyone who could be an eye in the sky observing us, and listening to this conversation, would see a very capable, normal person who excels in his day-to-day life. Anyone listening to your reasoning ability, your superior communications skills and hyper-intelligence would be more than impressed. However, anyone listening to you say that you morphed into a mongoose to fight a snake would have you committed. You are still claiming you have these supernatural powers. What else have you morphed into? Where else have you gone?"

"I can also morph into inanimate objects. I changed into a soccer ball at Em's game and helped her score two goals."

"Zachary, you poor thing, you were sitting next to me the whole time."

"I have the ability to morph into other people or objects while I retain my original shape and thoughts."

Daphne kicks the chair backward with her foot and stands up. "Okay, here's the deal. You have two choices. One, you show me some example of this great power. Power, yes, that's what you call it, PowZak. Either you show me and Dr. Principo an example, or I will ask him to put you in a facility where you can be observed and treated. I will notify IBX of the details, and force them to fire you. If this continues, you are going to blow yourself up. I have you and this family to protect. Your move, Zachary." Daphne doesn't stop to think whether she is doing the right thing from a therapist's point of view. She has reached the limits of her tolerance.

"What if I give you an end date? By that I mean the time when all research on PowZak is completed."

"Not good enough. You would tell me it was completed when it wasn't, and still be infected with delusional thoughts that you kept quiet. That would be even worse, because it would be corrosive, and there is no telling what you might do. You must be free of all these delusions. Either show me now or be treated. Right fucking now, Zachary."

"You mentioned my showing you *and* Dr. Principo. In three days I have a session with him. He wants me to meet a colleague of his, a doctor named Pierre Toussaint. Can you wait until then for proof of my abilities?" He desperately tries to buy himself some time.

"You talked about an end date. That is your end date, Zachary. It ends one way or the other on Tuesday. I was going to take Em and Ethan to Mom's house, but I don't want to upset them. You are going on a business trip. You will leave late this afternoon. Pack your suitcase, load up your car. You will not sleep in our bed again until this is resolved. I've had it."

«««‹›»»»

Zachary is driving his new Volkswagen EOS down Interstate 89 toward the New Hampshire border, with no particular destination in mind. He gathered his computer, his amplifiers and frequency generators, the PowZak formula and the antidotes, and stowed them in the trunk. He said a quick goodbye to the children and told them he'd had a phone call from work: He had to be in Boston for a meeting Monday morning, and there was no time to book a flight. His boss wanted to go over details at the hotel on Sunday. It was a good story, told convincingly because he didn't want to upset them. Daphne was equally convincing for the same reason.

He'd thought that eventually he would have to take one of two paths. The first was to continue with PowZak research. The second was to abandon it completely and never mention it again. Now things have changed. He no longer has these options. He must either prove his claims about the drug's power or be faced with his wife and therapist demanding hospital treatment. He would lose his job, and his personal and family life would probably never recover.

The discovery and perfection of PowZak had become a quest, as important to him as the Holy Grail was to its pursuers in antiquity. Now it felt more like an albatross around his neck, dragging him down as it did the Ancient Mariner in Coleridge's poem. He's acting like the character in Edward Randall's story. Ralph rubbed it on his car's fender to fix the dents, and he thought about cloning fifty-dollar bills. Zachary doesn't think he has done much better. He morphed into a soccer ball to help his daughter score goals. He chose to become a fly and a flea and a sow bug. Perhaps it was time to give up the entire project and hand it over to Cornell. He could give some small proof to his wife and to the doctors that would show, without any doubt, that PowZak works. He could then put it into Principo's hands, with instructions to present the whole mess to the University, and walk away.

I can't do it. I can't just walk away. How does a mother leave a beloved child? How does a man leave a home he has built from the first brick? How does he cast himself off into the night and become homeless?

Zachary realizes that he has *four* options. The first is to admit that he is delusional and submit himself for treatment, keeping PowZak a secret. He would keep his wife and family, but lose his job. The second is to continue his research and abandon his therapy and family, and also probably his job. The third is to show them what it can do, and continue his research. This is the most dangerous of all options, because he seriously doubts if they can handle it. The fourth is that everything goes to Cornell, himself included. He would lose his job and have to live near the university.

Oh shit, Em is going to ask Daphne what hotel I'm staying at in Boston. Daphne won't know what to say. I hate lies. You tell one, and before you know it there's another, and then another to keep the line of deception in order. We have caller ID, so I can't fake the call from someplace else.

Zachary uses his cellphone to call Daphne. "I'll be brief. I'm afraid Em might want to call me, or expect a call from the hotel. I'm planning to stay at the Sheraton in Boston and walk around the city."

"I told her you were staying at the Hyatt. Go there instead. Please be careful."

"I'm sorry, Doctor, I know I did the wrong thing. I can't handle it anymore. I can't listen to him talk, straight-faced, about turning into a mongoose and fighting a pit viper after, of course, morphing from a parrot. Yet he continues to be loving, worrying about Em not knowing where he really is."

"I know, please try to calm yourself. He wrote the same story for me. That's why I voiced concern at our last meeting. Has he called from Boston?"

"Last night. After he spoke to Em and Ethan, I brought the phone into the bedroom. We had a tearful conversation. He apologized for putting me in such a horrible position, as he put it, and said he had reached a decision on what to do. He will tell us at tomorrow's session."

"I have thoroughly briefed Dr. Toussaint. His advice will be invaluable. No one in the country knows more about delusional disorder than he does. Did I ever show you his books?" Dr. Principo walks across the room to his library and chooses three sizeable texts on the subject. "So you see, Daphne, Pierre literally wrote the book. He was one of the people who pioneered the early research in the 1970s. I know this is very difficult, but please try to have faith that we will find a way to help your husband. Has he discussed any aspect of his childhood, or did you remember anything of value?"

"Not much, really. He had a twin brother who died in the car crash. Zachary was the only one of his family who survived it. He was only two years old: I don't see how he could remember. He never talks about his aunt or his family."

"Twin brother! Twin brother!" Dr. Principo throws his pen into the air. "Of course he remembers! This is great, Daphne! This is great news!" The doctor is very excited and chokes on a nut tart. He drinks a cup of coffee. "This could explain why he is trying to be someone else. He could be attempting to recapture the lost soul that was his brother. Twins share a special bond. A piece of him has been missing, so instead of creating an alter-ego, he has morphed into another version of himself. I can't wait to tell Pierre."

«««‹›»»»

Dr. Pierre Toussaint is a short man, five foot five. He has dark bushy eyebrows and a full head of naturally black hair that is interesting when combined with his weather-beaten face. He is in his late seventies, but looks ten years younger. He doesn't smile often and, as a matter of fact, looks rather dour most of the time.

Daphne is so nervous that her teeth are chattering. She refused to take a Valium, wanting to be in complete control of her powers without dumbing them down. Even the usually upbeat Dr. Principo sits in nervous anticipation of Zachary's visit. The session was supposed to start at seven p.m., and it is now five minutes to the hour.

"Please let him do the taking," Dr. Toussaint advises Daphne. I know you are heavily involved, but we must let him tell us what he has decided. This will give us a clue how we are to proceed with this visit. I must stress that there is a big difference between the treatment protocol for here and now, and the path we will take for future therapy."

"I will sit and listen, unless he says something that I know to be untrue."

"No, no!" Toussaint is emphatic. "Do not challenge him on any issue or on any level. He must have complete freedom to say whatever he wants to whomever he wants. This is vital."

The clock now reads 7:15. "Son of a bitch is late," Daphne says. She gets up and paces back and forth in front of the bookcase. "What are we to do if he doesn't show up?"

"It would be completely out of character for him not to show up. I suggest we wait. He is late, that is all," Dr. Principo says, trying to convince himself that his patient will keep the appointment. The clock now reads 7:30.

"Good evening, everyone." Zachary's voice is clearly heard in the room.

Dr. Principo turns to face the door to his study, but Zachary is not standing in the entryway. The doctor gets up and looks down the hall, but there is no one there.

"What the hell did he do, smuggle in a tape recorder on a timer? Where did he put it? This is a rotten joke for him to play on us, a rotten joke."

"I don't play rotten jokes. You wanted proof, and now you have proof."

"What kind of proof? There is no proof. All you did is hide a transmitter and receiver somewhere in my office. I will find it, and you will still have to talk to us. Where the hell are you?"

"Dr. Toussaint, pleased to meet you. I like the French tooled leather belt you have on. The buckle is made of sterling silver. Was it a gift from your son? You don't see him very often any more, do you?"

Dr. Toussaint rises from his chair and looks out the window into the darkness. "I don't see anything outside. Where could he have his camera? Where is the speaker?"

"Zachary, where the fuck are you?" Daphne screams.

Chapter Fifteen

It's nine o'clock in Dr. Principo's office, and Daphne and the two psychiatrists are recapping the events of one hour before.

"This is a good one, Antonio: we're dealing with a master." Dr. Toussaint is attempting to explain what just happened. "He played a game with us. Had us write down a number or a phrase on a piece of paper and hold it in front of our faces. We then heard his voice tell us what was on the three pieces of paper. No camera could have done that. He would have needed three cameras, one in each wall, and would have had to know beforehand where we would be sitting. No, absolutely impossible that it was a camera. And where did his voice come from? There was no discernible source."

"Could he have hypnotized me and Daphne?" Dr. Principo asks.

"It is remotely possible that he could have used hypnotic suggestion to cause you to write something that was preordained by his design, but the chances are so incredibly slim as to be off the charts. Plus, I had no contact with him whatsoever before this meeting. I still don't know what he looks like. Antonio, he is a master. I've seen people like him before; you think they are absolute magicians. To preserve his delusions, to keep from facing them, he has invented and created the most masterful ruse I have ever seen. I still don't know how he did the voice and the paper trick. Absolutely masterful!" Dr. Toussaint is looking for a scientific explanation.

"I'd better call the kids and tell them I'll be awhile." Daphne dials her home and Emma answers. "Hello Em, I'm going to be a little late. Oh, when did he arrive? Thanks for telling me, honey. I'll be there very soon.

"That was my daughter Emma. Zachary has been home since six-thirty. He has been in the living room with the children watching television. He told her to tell me that he loved me and not to worry because all will be well. Any theories?"

"Absolutely masterful," Pierre Toussaint says again as he slaps his knee. "I insist on working with you on this case. There is no way we should even think about hospitalization. He can do whatever he wants. There isn't a facility in the world that has a staff that can match wits with your husband. We have to uncover his delusions one on one. Daphne, let's find out what he tells you about missing this session. After all, he wasn't here. How will he explain it? And, when he does appear for a session without you, Daphne, how will he react to the mention of his childhood and to his twin? I want to gauge his reaction when we further discuss his paper-and-sound trick. I have to know how he did that. I absolutely have to know."

Zachary is lying on the bed. When Daphne walks into the room, he jumps up, puts his finger to his lips and says, "Shush, please don't shout. Don't say anything. I know you said I can't sleep in this bed until things are resolved. We must do this one step at a time. This is the first step. I want to talk to you about what just happened. Will you listen without losing your temper?"

Daphne nods her head yes. He throws his arms around her but she pushes him away. "Daphne, I heard everything that you and the doctors said. I heard Dr. Toussaint talk about my masterful ruse. I heard the three of you question whether or not I used hypnotic suggestion. I'm going to tell you how I did it. You need to be brought in slowly or it will be too traumatic."

"Okay, Zachary, your speech is wonderful, as usual. How did you do the magic trick?"

"Did you notice anything unusual about the room?"

"For Christ's sake, Zachary, we went over every inch of that room twenty times. That's why I'm asking you how you did it. I hope you feel ashamed that you are making fools out of some fine men who just want to help you, not to mention a wife who loves you."

"It's always once removed, isn't it? You can never show me, in front of my face, a tangible example of your PowZak. Now you're a fly again. Aren't you aware that you are using one of the biggest clichés ever invented, a fly on the wall? You're forgetting something, Mister Scientist: I'm an empath, and I can read you like a book, if I may throw another cliché at you. I know when someone is lying, and...."

"So, am I lying?"

"No, you're not, but that's because you're delusional. I don't have the faith that your therapists have in arriving at the root causes by examining your childhood. I believe in changing behavior. Changing the way you think and react will eventually cause a change in your symptoms, and believe me, you have some dandies. I will not pussyfoot around you, my love. When you deal with me, you will be challenged on every syllable you utter. A fly on the fucking wall!

"Zachary, I'm not asking you to leave, but our relationship is going to change. It's already changed. I don't trust you anymore. Perhaps you don't think that's important. So, if you want that kind of marriage, you got it. You just hang on to your fly on the wall, and see how much comfort that gives you, you shithead.

"Sometimes I wonder if therapy is any use at all. I suppose it works somewhat with troubled middle-school kids, but if the Sidtherns are any example of...." Daphne runs out of the living room, down the hall, grabs her cellphone, and runs into the garage.

"Hello, Dr. Principo. I'm sorry, I didn't know you were in a therapy session, but I know how he did it. You have a light fixture on the ceiling in the center of your study, don't you? Check it out right away for a miniature camera. I'll bet he used the Sidtherns as a model for his ruse. If you climb a stepladder and look inside the.... I don't care if it's a sealed globe light; it's easy to unscrew the glass. Somehow he found the time and opportunity to put a camera inside. One other idea: use gloves to open it. I want you to dust the glass for fingerprints. If he returned on the sneak to take the camera out, I'll bet you anything that his prints are all over it. I'll be right there."

"Zachary, I'm going out, and I don't know when I will be back." Daphne slams the back door and backs her car out of the garage. She drives to Dr. Principo's house in Charlotte. When she arrives, he and Dr. Toussaint are sitting in the study. A stepladder is in the middle of the floor, and the glass from the light fixture is sitting on the table next to the doctor's desk.

"There was no camera inside, and we're now dusting for prints. I know how to do this. You use either white or black powder, depending on the surface. I'm using black powdered charcoal. I have Zachary's diary, which he gives me every week. It will be very easy to match the prints."

First, Dr. Principo dusts the papers and produces three clear images of Zachary's fingerprints. Next, he dusts the light fixture glass and finds four distinct prints. They don't match Zachary's or the doctor's.

"They must be from the guy who installed it. You know there *is* something funny." He walks over to the wall switch and flicks it on and off. "The light works. I've never used it because it always flickered. I guess the bulb was loose. The guy who installed it must not have turned the new-style bulb in far enough, and it didn't make good contact. I like my floor and desk lamps better, so I never turned it on. I know I'm not PC, but I like the warm yellow color of the old-style bulbs. So why does the light work now, when it didn't work before?"

"Because no matter how careful and deliberate a delusional patient is trying to be, he can't rise above his obsessive compulsions," Dr. Toussaint interjects. "What we have here is circumstantial evidence, but it is still evidence. Very good, Daphne. You may have hit on the only explanation. We won't be fooled again. Don't lose patience. Our therapy must be very different from that used with a typical delusional patient. He shows no danger of turning violent, fleeing if challenged, or even regressing further into his delusions by our actions. Perhaps it's time to turn up the heat. This is what I suggest we do."

The temperature is unseasonably mild for early December, and Zachary is enjoying sitting on a cedar Adirondack chair that he brought out from the garage. He sets up two chairs side by side. The late afternoon sun is reflecting off the snow and feels warm on his face. Daphne sits next to him.

"No Daphne, I didn't use the Sidthern's camera as a model for my ruse. I didn't tamper with Dr. Principo's light fixture. It's easy to know what you're thinking. As soon as you mentioned the Sidtherns, you were off like a rabbit. I'm not a burglar who would break into his therapist's home. Give me credit for a little class. I know this is hard on you, and I'm going to continue to work with you. Do you like seagulls?"

"I wish I were married to one, Zachary. You really are annoying me. Looks like we're back to our constant warfare. I hope you're happy."

"Of course not. I don't want to fight, not at all." Zachary's voice is calming and reassuring. He slowly repeats the phrase, *Not at all, not at all.* "Let me introduce you to a friend of mine." A snow-white seagull with black wingtips lands on the picnic table five feet away from Daphne's chair. "Daphne, what would you like to have: a pinecone, a twig, a piece of bark, or a leaf?"

"I will admit that this bird is remarkably tame. They don't usually come in this close. You must have been feeding it."

"You didn't answer my question. What would you like to have?"

"A pinecone."

The seagull flies to the wooded border between the Warrens' and their neighbor's home, picks up a two-inch-long pinecone, flies to the arm of Daphne's chair, and drops it in her lap.

Zachary smiles. "Now what would you like to have: a paperclip, a piece of paper with the number 47 written on it, a green clothespin, or a nickel? If you look closely, you will see them on the ground at the water's edge, about ten feet from the pier. I have a rock on the paper to keep it from blowing away. Which one, Daffy?"

"The nickel," Daphne says with her voice high-pitched and shaky. The seagull flies to the water's edge and retrieves the nickel. Daphne is having an anxiety attack and is breathing very hard.

"Hold out your hand." She does as directed, but her hand is shaking. The bird drops the nickel into it and flies away across the lake. "Okay Daphne, what has happened here? Can you give me a rational explanation?"

"No."

"Would you say that this was an unusual happening?"

"Yes."

"Do you think it's possible that I selected a seagull at random and trained it to bring you those items by voice commands?"

"No, yes, I don't know."

"Can we go inside and shape the pizza dough? I'm hungry." Daphne doesn't move. Zachary picks her up out of the chair and carries her to the living room couch.

«««‹›»»»

"Dr. Principo, I have to see you right away, right away, right now! I'm sorry but I have to see you right now!"

Daphne holds out a trembling hand and gives a nickel to the doctor. "Zachary made a seagull land next to my chair. He then asked me if I wanted a twig, leaf, or a pinecone. I chose a pinecone and he made the seagull find one and drop it in my lap. He then asked me if I wanted a piece of paper, a nickel, a paperclip, and something else. They were on the bank by the water's edge. I chose the nickel, and the bird fetched it and dropped it in my hand. Doctor, am I going mad?"

"This is the nickel he...er...the seagull gave you?"

"Yes."

"What did he say to you just before the seagull did its tricks? How was his voice? Was he calm, was he excited?"

"He was very calm. What do you suspect?"

"I don't know for sure. Daphne, you may have been hypnotized."

"But why?"

"I don't know. Ask Zachary to call me when you get home. I'm going to change our appointment to tomorrow. We've got to get to the bottom of this quickly. I suggest you talk to your parents and have them stand by in the event that you and your children have to leave the house."

"Is it that bad, Doctor?"

"It could be. Promise me you will be careful."

The two doctors confer about Daphne's recent experience, and Dr. Principo decides to ask an old friend for help. He makes the call from his study in the presence of Dr. Toussaint.

"Pierre, I'm going to call Dr. John O'Hara. He's the Director of Library Sciences at UVM. I have an idea."

"Hello John, this is Antonio. How the hell are you? I know it's been awhile. Could you do me a big favor? I know you can't release the particulars of who checks out what unless you have an order from the FBI. I have a patient who may be engaging in illegal activity and harming his family and I wonder if you could make an exception. As you probably surmised, I can't yet go to the police. All I want to know is if this individual has taken out any books recently, and if so, what. Thanks a million, John. His name is Dr. Zachary Warren. Sure, I'll be here all afternoon. Talk to you soon."

"Hello, John. You have some information? He took out four books on hypnosis. What are the titles? I owe you big-time. You may have saved a family from untold grief."

"Pierre, I see him tonight. I am going to confront him with my knowledge. Let's see how he attempts to wriggle out of this one."

«««◇»»»

"Zachary, come in. I asked you to change your appointment because I'm concerned about something important."

"Daphne told you about the seagull. I knew she would. As I said before, I must introduce all of you to PowZak very slowly, in small degrees, or the result will be too traumatic."

"Tell me something, Zachary. In your reading or studies, have you ever had occasion to research hypnosis?"

Zachary suspects that his doctor may have newly discovered knowledge of his book-reading patterns. "As a

204

matter of fact, I have done some recent reading on the subject. I've checked a few books out of the UVM library. I suspected that you and Dr. Toussaint were going to recommend hypnosis as part of my treatment to unlock my childhood memories, and I wanted to learn more about it so I could make an informed decision. Why do you ask?"

«««‹›»»»

"Daphne, who handles the finances in your family, you or Zachary?" Dr. Principo is on the phone with Daphne. He suggested she pull her car off the road lest she become distracted by their troubling conversation. It is snowing and the sound of the SUV's windshield wipers can clearly be heard by the doctor.

"Zachary does. He's the scientist with the best head for math. It was mostly all his aunt's money. We keep a flex CD at the bank, and I can draw out as much as I need."

"If you don't mind my asking, how much is in the flex CD?

"About forty thousand dollars."

"Do you know how much money you have in the other accounts?"

"No."

"Could you find out for me?"

"What do you suspect?"

"I'm not sure. I'm trying to piece together behavior patterns that might possibly make some sense. As his wife, you have every right to the information. Ask him where he keeps the rest of his money and how much there is. You are scheduled to see me tomorrow. I have some news about what happened to you and that seagull. Call me when you find out about the finances."

Daphne calls the Volkswagen dealership and asks them if there was a problem with her husband's check. She claimed he'd asked her to make sure there were sufficient funds. They informed her that the check, from Green Mountain Savings and Loan, cleared without a problem. She now knows there is a second account at the bank, and it is in her husband's name. She knows the bank won't tell her how much is in it.

"Zachary, I was wondering something. You wrote a check to Volkswagen from another account at the bank, not from our flex CD. Why is this account in only your name, and how much is in there?"

"Oh, that's not important, just an oversight on my part. I will be happy to call them tomorrow and turn it into a joint account. You will be able to access it at any time. What's mine is yours, you know." Zachary smiles.

"How much is in there?"

"About eighty thousand dollars."

"Where else do you have *our* money invested, and how much is there?" Daphne shakes the snow from her L.L. Bean goose-down parka and hangs it on a hook in the mudroom next to the garage.

"Good heavens, I have all sorts of investments. I have to wait for the next quarterly statements to let you know the exact amounts."

"Approximately how much, and where is it invested? Do you use a brokerage house, or do you handle them yourself? Do you have bonds or other savings accounts? May I see the last quarterly statements? I have a right to know."

"Wow, all of a sudden you have a million questions. You don't trust my financial management? Have you ever wanted for anything?"

Chapter Sixteen

"I have wonderful news. But first I want to talk with you about Zachary. Daphne, please sit down. How is his treatment progressing? I know you love him, but I don't trust that man." Mildred Pettersen speaks forcefully.

"We're having problems, as usual. This is a difficult time, and we'll have to see what happens. Please don't interfere."

"Always remember, you and the children are welcome here. If you divorce, you will probably have to sell the house."

"Mom, let's not go there. There is a vast territory ahead. What's the good news?"

Daphne's father walks into the living room and sits on the long couch, on the other side of his daughter. He is holding a large envelope, and he takes out multicolored stock certificates and legal papers with official seals. Flanked now by her parents, Daphne receives strong signals of impending delight.

"Daughter, we are rich."

"Rich?"

"Rich."

"How rich?"

"Well, there's rich, very rich, and super or filthy rich. We're in the last category. Let me tell you what happened. As you know, your grandfather died two years ago. It seems he had a fortune socked away. It was held up in Norwegian courts. I never had any idea of his holdings, and I received a communication from a Norwegian attorney late yesterday. Pop had a sizeable share of Nokia and owned a portion of Fiat in Italy. I don't know why he kept it a secret. The taxes are complicated, involving three countries, but our attorney says we should realize about 120 million dollars cash in American funds after all the taxes and attorney fees are paid.

"The money will be available in two or three weeks. You are our only heir. What do you think of that? I don't know quite how to handle this."

"I do," Mildred Pettersen says. "Daphne, I won't give you any money as long as you're married to *him*."

"You can do better than that. You don't know me at all, do you? I don't give a shit if you inherited 120 *billion* dollars. That's a cheap way to attempt to exert control over my life. Keep your God-damned money and leave me alone!"

"Now Daphne, your mother's just trying to help. She has your best interests at heart." Her father chases after her as she storms out of the house.

«««‹›»»»

"Daphne, this is wonderful news about your family's good fortune. Does Zachary know about it?"

"I don't see how he could. My father learned only yesterday. This is privileged information. Zachary couldn't possibly know. Why, do you think he is trying to drive me mad to collect my family fortune? That's a bit far-fetched."

"Perhaps," Dr. Toussaint says, "but the reason Dr. Principo and I are having such a difficult time analyzing his delusions is that there may not be any. It's entirely possible he is faking the condition for another ulterior motive. All of a sudden, the news of your family money surfaces. I don't like coincidences. As Sherlock Holmes once said, to arrive at the truth you must strip away that which is not true, or something like that."

"Do you still think I was hypnotized? I can remember everything that happened the whole time I was sitting in the chair."

"Yes, it's possible," Dr. Principo responds. "Let me tell you about hypnosis. When you are in a trance, which is really semi-conscious relaxation, you still maintain sensory contact with your immediate environment. Most of the time the trance is induced by a therapist, or other person, repeating words or phrases in a calm, rhythmic way. You told us that Zachary spoke in a calm, possibly repetitive voice. Once in a trance, the subject is highly suggestible. he has higher intellectual functioning, his memory can be tapped, and thoughts put into his consciousness.

"What happens is the ARF, that's the Ascending Reticular Formation area of the brain, is bombarded by the hypnosis, and there is a sensory decoupling. The subject is alert and not asleep. Only highly ethical therapists can be trusted to use hypnosis. It is entirely possible that Zachary convinced you, under hypnosis, that you saw a seagull bring you those objects. Done for his own motives, that was *not* ethical.

"Daphne, I know for a fact that Zachary checked out four books on hypnosis from the UVM library. I have a friend at the school who told me; it is beyond a shadow of a doubt. I must admit I was flatfooted when I confronted him. I shouldn't have come right out and asked him if he had studied hypnosis. Naturally, he knew that I must have some knowledge or I wouldn't have asked the question. He answered that he checked them out because he wanted to learn about the subject in the event we used the technique to unlock his childhood memories. It seems that he's always one step ahead of us."

"There is another possibility here," Dr. Toussaint interjects. "He may be learning about the subject as a protective device. There are so many layers in this case and trying to unravel them all, the facts, the theories, the possible motivations, is making my head spin. This is what an advanced delusional patient does. When there is smoke and mirrors, and confusion, the truth will be obfuscated. Daphne, Dr. Principo and I are suggesting a very risky form of treatment. It's not risky for Zachary, but for us. We wondered how you would feel about our hypnotizing him. We could ask key questions and discover information that we could never otherwise unlock. I admit that this is usually not done with delusional patients, and the chances for success with Zachary are probably slim. He would have to be told beforehand."

"If you feel it would help, you certainly have my blessing. Why would it be risky for you?"

"Risky in the sense of it not working. He has been doing extensive reading. He may be able to counter the hypnotic suggestions and resist trance. He is so very smart that we run that risk. I'm worried that he might not agree to it, end the therapy and communications would cease. You would be on your own. We are holding this card in reserve, only if nothing else works. Right now I'm concerned about his latest actions." Dr. Toussaint is somber.

"He knows. Believe me, he knows about your family money. We don't know how he knows, but he knows. He knows."

"Antonio, stop repeating the word *knows*. You are going to hypnotize Daphne."

Daphne doesn't smile at Pierre Toussaint's attempts at humor. "It doesn't make any sense for Zachary to fake a delusional condition. It also doesn't make any sense for him to pull another ruse, this time with a seagull. Sooner or later, the whole mess is going to backfire and blow up, and he knows it. There has to be another explanation. Is it possible, is it remotely possible, that he is telling the truth about PowZak?"

"Absolutely not," Dr. Principo says. "Do I have to remind us of all the creatures he has supposedly morphed into? Come on, a fly on the wall? The fact that you are considering that possibility, Daphne, shows that you are growing weary from the strain of it all. This is so understandable. You don't want to think ill of your husband if he *is* malevolent, or even admit that there is a high possibility that he is ill. You are too close to him to play an active part in any further therapy. It's not fair to you. I must insist that you take care of yourself and the children. I will continue to see you every two weeks, or more often if there is a crisis. I'll let you know if we decide to attempt hypnosis."

«««‹›»»»

"Daphne, I haven't been totally honest about our finances. I guess I've been somewhat ashamed."

"Oh, really, *somewhat* ashamed."

"I didn't inherit 5 million dollars from my aunt, just 2.5 million. We spent 1.5 on this house, bought a few fancy cars, and I spent some more on research projects. Right now our total cash assets are the flex CD account, 40 thousand dollars, 80 thousand in the other account, which is now a joint account, and 150 thousand dollars in these two mutual funds. There's 100 thousand in one and 50 in the other."

He puts the folders on the kitchen table. "I'm sorry I deceived you. I guess I lied to you because I wanted to impress you before we were married. I made some bad investments and lost money in the last stock downturn. We do have enough; we both make fine money. I make over a quarter of a million in salary, and even more in benefits. I have a great future at IBX. We can easily add to our nest egg."

"Is there anything else you would like to disclose? Extra-marital affairs, gambling addiction, drugs, compulsive lying?" Daphne knocks the mutual fund brochures off the table onto the floor. "Did it ever occur to you that your delusional episodes are endangering your position at IBX? This is a small town, and they are not going to advance a person whose marriage and social life are in turmoil."

"I do have something else to confess. I have been listening to your conversations."

"My God, Zachary, I can't wait to hear this one."

"I can enter into the spirit and mind of another person, and see what they can see, and hear what they can hear. I'm very proud of you for walking out on your parents. It proves beyond any doubt that you love me. I don't care about their money, either. I want you to draw up a legal paper that in the event of your death, or of our divorce, that all the money in our family, cash assets on hand, or inherited from your family, will revert back to your parents' management in trust for our children. Think of it as a post-nuptial agreement. I don't want one dime of their money, and I don't care if you inherit millions. I just want us to be happy. Money and power are anti-happiness."

"What about PowZak? How does that figure into your happiness quotient? How the hell did you hear our conversation? You were nowhere near my parents' house. Please don't tell me another fucking fly on the wall. Did you plant a bug on me? Christ, Zachary, you are not being kind. You are making me very unhappy. Please leave. Right now, please leave. I'm going to see a lawyer."

"No!" Zachary shouts, lifts Daphne up in the air and puts her down on the couch. "Not that."

"You have made your choice. You have chosen your PowZak delusions over your family. Now let me up."

Zachary has a tight grip around Daphne's middle and refuses to let go. "No, I don't make that choice. I'll let you make it for me. I knew it would come to this. You are too precious to be jerked around. Those two wonderful doctors are breathing down my neck. It's not fair to anybody. Please call and say we must see them right away, or at least ask them when the earliest convenient time would be." Zachary removes Emma's video recorder from the coffee table, makes it fly through the air, and land on Daphne's lap.

"No hypnosis, no tricks. We will bring this video recorder with us, and you and the doctors can film me. Please?"

"My God, you can move objects with your thoughts."

"I have to trust that you can handle what I am about to show you. We have a family to think about. I hope you're strong enough. The way things are going now, nothing could be much worse. Divorce? Not going to happen. It will be up to you and the doctors whether I am to continue with this research. I will defer to your judgment for the sake of our family. I can no longer make this decision alone. I'm sorry I ever discovered the fucking shit."

"He can see us right away," Zachary says after calling the doctor. "I'm going to leave a note for Em and ask her to call for pizzas at seven. We should be through by then. Daphne, grab the camera. Let's go.

"I love driving through the snow, especially in your car. What I'm doing now, Daphne, is entering into the mind of

Dr. Toussaint. He has just had a rapprochement with his son. He is waiting for us, but his thoughts are of buying a cottage here in Vermont to be close to his family. He's thinking of buying a summer camp on Grand Isle. The house is blue with a wonderful view of the bay. He is going to suggest a trial separation so you can be free of anxiety, and I can undergo the needed treatment, as they see it. Naturally I would lose my job, something I'm not willing to do. You see, Daphne, I do not have delusional disorder. I'm basically just a brilliant pain in the ass. You will soon see. You're holding the camera in your lap. You know how it got there. There's more to come, my love, much more."

«««‹›»»»

"He made this camera fly through the air and land in my lap. We had better listen to what he has to say." The two doctors and the Warrens are sitting in the combination study and therapy room .

"If the three of you are in agreement, I would like to use this camera to record our session. I have it set to a wide-angle view, so the entire room will be captured. Dr. Principo, do I have your permission to remove this bust of Dr. Freud and put the camera in its place on the bookshelf? It's the perfect height, and I don't have a tripod. Would either of you like to examine the camera to see if there is anything pre-recorded?"

"That isn't necessary. It will be easy to see if the recording is genuine. We do have the ability to remember what has been discussed, and who did what. What do you intend to prove by making a recording?" Dr. Toussaint is suspicious and untrusting of Zachary.

"The recorded mini-disk will be left with you to analyze. Is that acceptable?"

"Of course it is. Please proceed."

"Dr. Toussaint, Zachary told me that he can enter the minds and thoughts of others. He knew everything that we discussed in this room. He also knew the exact words of the argument I had with my parents. He was nowhere near my parents' house. I assure you that neither I nor the house have been bugged."

"Why are you so sure of that, Daphne? He could have done it."

"Doctor, I'm glad that you patched things up with your son. I know it has been on your mind. That blue house on Grand Isle would be perfect for a summer getaway. I also like the stained glass around the edge of the picture window facing the lake. I know you are going to suggest a trial separation so you can isolate Daphne from me. You will be, of course, trying to find a logical explanation for how I know these facts. Let me get right to it."

"There is always a logical explanation," Dr. Toussaint interjects. "You obviously had me followed. Are the stakes that high?"

Zachary removes one of Dr. Principo's books from the shelf and causes it to spin in the air above everyone's head. He then makes it land gently on the corner of the desk. Dr. Principo drops his nut tart.

"Listen carefully. I bear no animosity toward either of you fine men. Quite the opposite. You are acting on evidence the only way that seems logical. Throughout history, scientists have made judgments on the basis of what they know to be empirical laws. Whether it's diseases of the body or the mind, or of nuclear-chemical reactions, what has been previously discovered and known forms the basis of scientific logic.

"Neither of you can formulate any theories about forces over which you have no knowledge or control. You are looking for a camera in a light fixture, books on hypnosis, financial explanations, and other blind alleys. You are attributing evil motivations to me that are too horrible to contemplate. You are looking for a solution that you will not find using any frame of reference that is part of your current scientific knowledge.

"I can freely walk away from these sessions at any time without any further contact or explanation. You cannot stop me legally, or in any other way. However, I'm not going to do this because our dialogue (and that's what it is, good doctors, a dialogue, it is not therapy) is important to me and to my family. I guess in a way it *is* therapeutic. I really do need your counsel to help me sort it all out, but for Christ's sake, I am not delusional. Dr. Toussaint, you already know that, and you're looking for other explanations, mostly trying to substantiate your theories about diabolical actions on my part.

"I have made many mistakes, more than can be covered in this session. I am guilty of bad financial management, but that is all. You have convinced Daphne, by implication, that I am after her family fortune. Just before we arrived here, she wanted to send me away for good, and talked about divorce. I guess I had to have an ultimatum from her before I faced what is really important in my life. I've made my choice, and now I'm going to tell you what it is.

"But before we decide what to do, you must know what's at stake here, and whether or not you want to take it on. You have to understand that PowZak is so important that it transcends everything that we have discussed. It is bigger than either of you, of me, of my family, of her fortune, of our marriage, potential divorce, happiness or tranquility, of anything!" Zachary is raising his voice and his face is turning quite red.

"Zachary, calm down and tell us more about your work," Daphne says in a reassuring manner.

"In the past, I felt that the study and perfection of PowZak must come first, no matter how painful it was for me to make that choice. I will now leave it in your hands, the three of you. If you want me to abandon the project, I will do it. If you want me to pass it on to Cornell University, I will do it. If you want me to continue with my work, and assist me in the process, then that will be our direction. Everything I have done has been documented and can be replicated. I put no time limit on your decision, but I prefer to know your decision as soon as possible."

With his thoughts, Zachary takes two more books from the shelves and places them on top of the first book on the corner of the desk. He makes all three spin in a parabolic orbit above their heads. He then returns them to the shelves.

"My God, he is absolutely masterful," Dr. Toussaint says.

"I will see you next week with more demonstrations and evidence of PowZak. I prefer if Daphne is included in the sessions." He walks over to the video recorder, removes the mini-disk, and hands it to Dr. Principo.

"Thank you for your patience, good doctors. No pun intended."

Chapter Seventeen

"What else can you do besides make objects move?"

The snow is deep, and the SUV is plowing through it. Zachary is moving his head from side to side in time with the windshield wipers. He is humming a Scarlatti etude and is smiling.

"You know, Daphne, this is the first time in many months that I have felt free and liberated. We have so much to do and experience together. If you could change into anything you wanted, what would it be?"

"Zachary, you *are* serious. I'm not ready for this. I'm still not convinced that all this is real. What did you have in mind, change me into a sow bug?"

"You must progress at your own pace, if you want to do it at all. If you want to consult with the doctors first, I completely understand. I will not put pressure on you. If you want me to show you more of what PowZak will do strictly as an observer, than that's what we'll do."

"That's a great idea. That's what I want. I would like to see more evidence of PowZak. When can we do it? Zachary...Zachary!" Daphne is shouting, but there is no one sitting beside her. The steering wheel is turning by itself. "Zachary, Zachary, come back!"

He reappears, grinning like a Cheshire cat. "Sorry to startle you, but I've been wanting to do that for a long time."

"Oh my God, you made yourself disappear. Why didn't you do it in front of the doctors?"

"They are not young men, and I didn't want to scare them."

"So you scare the shit out of me instead!"

"I'm sorry. Would you like me to do that at our next session? I could disappear, and then morph into other beings and objects. I'll let them know what I'm going to do before I do it, to lessen the shock. They will have everything on camera, and it will put an end, once and for all, to the conjecture about PowZak. Do you have anything you would like me to do, I mean besides make love to you as soon as we get home?"

"I don't want to wait until we get home. We'll scare the children."

Daphne makes Zachary pull off the road into an office parking lot. It is empty except for one vehicle, and the snow is falling heavily. Millions of swirling specks are beautifully illuminated by the downcast floodlights. They park at the far end, fold down the rear seat, and fog up all the windows.

Fifteen minutes later Daphne asks, "Why did you shut the engine off? I'm freezing my tutu." She places the emergency wool blanket around herself. Zachary starts the car from the back seat and turns on the heater.

"How did you do that?"

"God, I feel so liberated. We'd better get dressed. The heater will defog the windows, and we'll make quite a spectacle. We already have a reputation with the Shelburne Police. Perhaps this time they will throw us in jail for public indecency."

《《《〈〉》》》

"You two seem to be in a good mood for a change," Emma says, as her parents take off their boots in the mudroom. "I ordered the pizzas and here they are."

"Oh friggin' yum yum, this is even better than a dildo," Zachary says as he takes a huge bite out of a garlic and mushroom slice, to the delight of Ethan, who cackles.

"Language, Zachary, language."

«««◇»»»

"No Antonio, I don't think so. Yes, he has proven that he can move objects. I've never seen anything like it. I agree that it's documented, and it is not a ruse. We could never convince our colleagues that the video is real. I don't believe there is another example anywhere in the world, of someone moving three books in a perfect parabolic orbit. If I wasn't present while it was happening, I never would have believed it. To remove and then return them to your shelves requires mental powers that have not yet been documented. This is probably the very first time in human history. That alone is frightening. But I am not convinced about PowZak. Let me tell you why.

"First of all, there may still be a rational explanation: using double exposures, digital manipulation, multiple projectors, and other techniques that could have produced the images in the room and on that video recorder. How the hell should I know how he smuggled them in! If a person picks up a golf ball and throws it across the room, you and I would correctly assume that he has the power to throw that object. If, however, he then claims that he can lift and throw a pickup truck, a bus, or an ocean liner, and heave it across town, using his golf ball as proof, what do we then postulate?"

"I agree with you, Pierre. Just because he can move objects, it is not proof of all the other outlandish claims. Telekinesis is possible, even to such an advanced degree. After all, he does have remarkable intelligence. But changing into a fly on the wall is quite another matter. Let's formulate strategy for next week's session. Daphne is scheduled to see me alone just before we see him. I wonder if we could persuade Zachary to give a demonstration of his telekinesis at the University of Vermont?"

"Antonio, how's this for an idea. Zachary seems willing to offer us proof. He's now very much aware that Daphne has reached the end of her patience, no pun intended. At this point, it would help us if we had more witnesses. Why don't we propose that he offer us proof in front of other experts? We could do it here or at the university. I wonder if he will agree to it? If we go it alone, we will question our own sanity."

"Good idea, it's worth investigating. Don't forget, he did say that he had documentation and that every experiment could be replicated. Perhaps he will show us this documentation. I guess we need to get his approval first, about expanding the panel. I'll contact him *before* next week's session."

"No, Dr. Principo, I don't want to expand the panel or go to the university. I refuse to be a freak on parade. I am counting on your protection and upholding the sanctity of doctor-patient privacy. My job at IBX will be in jeopardy if word gets out about these experiments. They will wonder if I used their facilities, which of course I partly did, to create the drug. They will then claim ownership. Believe me, none of us wants a huge corporation like IBX to be in control over life and death. That is part of my problem, and why I'm so tortured about the discovery. I am equally hesitant to give it to Cornell. The U.S. Government would seize it in no time. Don't forget, I've worked with the NSA and hold a top secret clearance. I know what they're capable of.

"Is there anyone, is there any group in any agency or university who can make sound judgments under these circumstances? Everyone has an agenda. I tried to be pure and objective, and it was too much for me. It will be too much for you as well. Perhaps it's best if it's destroyed. But wouldn't that be the crime of the millennium? Welcome to my quandary. You'd better have something strong to wash down those nut tarts in our next session, Doc. It's going to get very interesting."

«««‹›»»»

Zachary is looking over Emma's shoulder. She is texting with her Huckleberry, as he calls it. "What's 2S2T, LOL?"

"Aw Dad, can't I have any privacy? It means too soon too tell, laugh out loud."

"What's so funny?"

"Privacy, a little privacy please."

"Her friend Janis has a new boyfriend," Daphne rolls her eyes. Emma runs out of the kitchen carrying her Huckleberry and shuts the door to her room.

"Here I am, about to turn thirty-seven in a few weeks, and I feel like an alien. I have an idea. First a little background. I've been doing some research. Did you know that girls Em's age are the supreme queens of texting? They send an average of 3,952 messages per month. That's not per year, that's per *month*." Zachary does quick division in his head. "That's about 132 per day. That's what she's doing right now. I'm convinced that texting is an infection. Sexting, for sure is an infection, but so is texting. All they do is sit there holding these devices. They send photos, videos, and messages while they are eating, driving, or walking. So help me, they probably send and receive them while they're sleeping."

"In my school we had to fail five kids who were taking an algebra test. They were texting the answers back and forth. The teacher caught them and confiscated their phones. It's an even bigger problem in the high school. My father told me that he's outlawed all cellphone and texting during classes. He said that when the end of period bell rings, they all run out into the halls and reach into their pockets. It's so funny because some of the kids who are texting each other are only a few hundred feet apart."

"You have got to be kidding me." Zachary is surprised.

"There's more. I'm counseling a little girl who just turned thirteen. She has been the object of bullying. They use the damned things to form sinister groups that belittle and exclude other kids. Can you believe it? Cyber-bullying. In spite of all the negative press, threats, and press coverage, they still send nude photos of themselves to each other. Not so much in my middle school, but definitely in the high school. They have no idea what can happen if those transmissions fall into the wrong hands. It could keep them from entering college or finding a decent job. They can get into legal or police trouble, especially the older kids. I agree with you, it *is* an infection. I hate them. But here I am using a cellphone. So what's your idea?"

"Do you remember how Em scored those goals in the soccer game? She's a great player, but she received a little help from her father. I can morph into any object while still retaining my original self in real time."

"Oh, not again, Zachary. How can you do this?"

"It's fairly complicated. I learned how to alter cells after they had split. The end result is that the host who has taken PowZak can then spin himself off into another entirely different entity without altering his original form. You then have two separate and different changlings that originated from the same root. The process is controlled by the original host, and the changlings can be animal, vegetable, or mineral. The second changling can create a third, the third a fourth, and so on. The host can reproduce exactly what is in his mind. I've computed a chart that uses amplitude and frequency to control the electrical stimulation needed.

"Look at this device." Zachary takes out a small object about the size of a cigarette lighter. "It took me a month to build it. It's a frequency generator and amplifier. Notice the two electrodes that retract into the bottom. It uses two common watch batteries. I also have a portable kit with PowZak that I can administer in any degree. I did notice some side effects of the drug. Actually, you did as well when you said that even my back was hard. For a while there I thought I was going down the same road as poor Gregor Samsa, in Kafka's *Metamorphosis*, and was going to turn myself into a cockroach. I increased the amount of compound A antidote, and the side effects have disappeared. But even after taking the antidote, I'm retaining some of the powers. I don't know where this will lead.

"You wanted to see more examples of PowZak, so this is what I propose. I am going to morph into a device just like Em's Huckleberry. Although these kids target specific URLs, namely their friends, I will be able to text all of them at once. I will be able to read everything and send counter messages. I intend to have some fun. Your job, Daphne, is to replace Em's Huckleberry with my device when the timing is right."

"You *are* serious."

"What's wrong with this thing? What's that supposed to mean? Hello Janice, did it show up on yours as well? Oh my God, it's on his too. Let's call Carol and Jimmy and see if they also got it. I have no idea what it means. It says URRTEL. PDYB&GAL. UHSWTD."

Two hours later the translation appears on all the devices: *You are ruining the English language. Put down your Huckleberries and get a life. You have schoolwork to do.*

The next morning at breakfast, Emma walks into the kitchen holding her Huckleberry. She is ignoring her family and is texting her friends.

"Is something the matter, Em?" Daphne asks.

"Something weird is happening to all our phones. Every kid in the school got the same message. First there was an abbreviation, and then it was translated."

"What was the translation?" Daphne asks.

"Put down your Huckleberries and get a life. You have school work to do."

"Bravo!" Zachary shouts. Daphne laughs.

Ethan shouts, "Dildo!"

"There's another message today. TIWNTOM. IWDSFSE. IWEHSIN,OASPTTW. Now what's that supposed to mean?"

Two hours later the translation appears on all the screens: *Today, I will not think of myself. I will do something for someone else. I will either help someone in need, or add something positive to the world.*

"Who could imagine? All our devices are infected with a virus!" Emma is animated and waving her arms.

"Doesn't sound like a virus to me. It sounds like an antidote and very sound advice," Zachary says with a mischievous laugh.

Emma puts her Huckleberry on the table and stands next to her father, who is eating an Eggo waffle. She gets two feet from him and stares at him without moving a muscle.

"You are responsible for this. I don't know how you are doing it, but I know you are the person who is putting out these messages. Do you deny it? You know it's wrong to lie to your children. You look at me and tell me the truth. Who else besides you calls these things Huckleberries?"

Zachary grins and doesn't look at Emma.

"Em, how could your father be responsible? He's sitting at the kitchen table eating a waffle. He may be smart, but not that smart."

"He's doing it. I know he's doing it. You'd better tell me."

"Em, we're going to be late for school. We can talk about this tonight."

When they are all together later in the day, on the sneak, Daphne takes Zachary's Blackberry out of Em's backpack and puts hers back in its place. She hands Zachary the morphed device. He places it on the kitchen table and turns it into a silver toast rack right in front of Daphne. He then makes the toast rack disappear.

"Daffy, darling, thanks for bailing me out with Em. She's not going to let this drop. She has the same empathic ability that you have. Actually, she's quite wonderful."

Emma and Ethan walk into the kitchen. "Dad, is Mom all right? She's pale and unsteady on her feet." Emma makes her mother sit down. "Are you pregnant?"

"No, I'm delusional. I need a vacation."

"Neat! When and where are we going?"

"Now, anywhere. Someplace warm. We can stay a couple of years. How about Saint Lucia? Look that up on your Huckleberry, Em, and let me know what you think."

«««‹›»»»

"All these therapists. I'm supposed to see Dr. Principo on Wednesday, and we have the Sidtherns tomorrow at seven.

233

They were checked out, and Dr. Principo found no evidence of wrongdoing. They're just kinky. Let's take the day off. Why don't we bring the kids to school, lock ourselves in the bedroom, and we won't come out until they get home.

"Zachary, I'm frightened, but I really want to be a part of these experiments. I can't believe the things I've seen with my own eyes. I've been questioning my sanity. I can do my crossword puzzles as usual, I can function perfectly well at work, as usual. I don't feel or believe that I'm acting like I'm nuts. How about it? We spend the day together tomorrow."

"Done. Let's call in sick."

The next morning, after driving the children to school, they are sitting on the living room couch.

"Our lovemaking is incredible. I didn't think it could be any better, but it keeps getting better. Is it the PowZak, Zak?"

"How would you like to find out?"

"What do you mean? I should take some before we make love? I'll do it, I'll do it. Right now!"

Zachary uses his atomizer and gives Daphne a medium dose of PowZak. He uses his GenAmp, the name he gave his electronic device, and places the electrodes on her wrist. He dials in the correct frequency and amplitude, and she feels a slight tingle.

"Now, you can do whatever you want and be whatever you want to be. What's neat here is that we can enter each other's minds and bodies. I've never done this before. Is there anything you would like to do, any fantasies that you want to live? If you can think it, you can be it."

"I always wondered what it would be like to make love like a man. But that would make you a woman."

"That's a great idea. I always wondered what it would feel like to be a woman. Let's go to bed."

"This is so strange, what's this large...Oh my God, you're me and I'm entering myself."

"No, that's not the spot, higher, higher," Zachary says as he gyrates under his wife's pounding.

"We're sorry, Ma'am, but we got another complaint." Zachary answers the front door when the Shelburne Police knock loudly. Since he's the man, it is his responsibility. He covers his lower half but forgets that he is now Daphne and must also cover his top. He quickly stands behind the door out of view of the police officers.

"Wait, let me guess, another passerby was walking her dog and thought there was a murder in progress."

"We're real sorry, Ma'am, but we had to check it out. We suggest soundproofing might help. Have a nice afternoon."

"Oh God, Em will be home in twenty minutes. Let's straighten up the bedroom. This place is a wreck." Zachary is apprehensive.

"I don't want to change back just yet. Can we stay like this for a while?" Daphne is enjoying her sex change. "Now I'm stronger than you are. I can throw you down on the bed like this, and....."

"Daphne, cut it out!"

Chapter Eighteen

Florence Sidthern is wearing a halter top, and Mitchell has on his favorite Hawaiian shirt. This is an odd choice of apparel since the outside temperature is minus seven.

"Please come in. I'm glad you didn't let that little rough spot at our last session stand in the way of your therapy. That was quite a snowstorm. We got about eighteen inches."

"I got only about six inches, in the back seat of my SUV," Zachary says, speaking in Daphne's body.

"So, how's work Zachary? I hear that you've made quite an impression at IBX."

"They love me because I'm so tall and manly. Actually, I'm quite a hunk, you know," Daphne says in Zachary's body, stroking her own chest.

"Excellent!" Florence claps her hands. "Everyone needs a good head of self esteem. How about you, Daphne, how have you and Zachary been getting along?"

"Great. I used to dish it out all the time: You know, thrust, thrust, thrust. It feels neat to be on the receiving end for once. I feel like I have all the power. I can make her...um...him do anything. But of course, I'm only attracting myself."

"Er, during lovemaking, which one of you initiates the action, or do you take turns?" Mitchell says with great curiosity.

"That depends," Daphne says. "When I'm him I sometimes do and when I'm me, I always do."

"I'm confused," Mitchell says. Have you been trying role reversal?

"Not at all, we're true hermaphrodites," Zachary says as he absentmindedly opens his legs to reveal his black lace underwear.

"Don't forget, it's about frequency and quality. You can't have one without the other," Mitchell says. "Do you dress in each other's clothes?"

"Oh, all the time. I have on the most delightful boxer shorts right now. What do you think of my cargo pants?"

Daphne says. "I can't get used to this thing," she says, grabbing her crotch. "Zachary, doesn't it get in the way?"

"No more than these two objects." He jiggles his breasts. "I'm always knocking things over when I turn suddenly."

"Um, that's a very good idea to try and identify with your spouse. That will lead to a greater understanding of each other's sexuality. Daphne, what do you find most interesting about male sexuality?" Mitchell asks.

"I like being the strong one. I won't take any shit and can throw him down on the bed. He was always lifting me up and carrying me around like a sack of potatoes, and now it's my turn." Zachary giggles at Daphne's comments.

"Er, I was asking Daphne, Zachary."

"She thinks she's now the strong one, but after she's finished, I can keep going. She can't wear me out, and I can make her tired and drain all her strength. I have all the power. Uh oh! What if I'm.....My God, Daphne, what if I made myself pregnant?"

"No, you didn't. I made *myself* pregnant. Let's get a testing kit to be sure," Daphne says as she folds her arms and crosses her legs, adjusting the cuff of her cargo pants.

"Have you two been taking any drugs?" Florence asks with enthusiasm. "If it's designer marijuana, would you be willing to sell us some?"

"Daphne, please come in. Please don't feel like we're ganging up on you," Dr. Principo says. "I asked Dr. Toussaint to be a part of this session. This is Special Agent Ron Krugman, from the FBI. I've been working with him on this case. We have worked together in the past...how many times, Ron, maybe a dozen? I've served as a special consultant to the agency."

"Uh, pleased to meet you. The FBI, why?"

"Dr. Principo correctly called us in because he suspected that a crime was being committed that may have crossed both state and international boundaries. We have been investigating your husband's activities for the last month. As you know, we cannot force a wife to testify against her husband, and that is not our intent here."

"You have no right to do anything. He hasn't committed any crimes. What kind of police state is this? Doctor, how could you? Zachary has discovered something that will change the world. How can you all be so blind?" Daphne is upset. "Just leave us alone! I'm out of here." She gets up from her chair and reaches for her coat.

"Just a minute, Daphne, please hear us out. You can make your decision after you learn the facts." Dr. Toussaint beckons her to sit back down. She reluctantly complies. "Agent Krugman will tell you what the FBI has discovered. It's important that you listen."

"Daphne, we know that your husband has been visiting MIT twice a week while employed by IBX."

"So big deal, is that a crime?"

"Nothing here by itself is necessarily a crime, but when the events are linked together it could point to wrongdoing. That's the key word here, Daphne, the word *could*. There is not yet any definitive proof. While at MIT, he used his excellent credentials to access their library, including the hundreds of doctoral dissertations. His main subjects of study, oddly enough, are not chemical or microbiology but miniature electronics and, this is most important, holography."

"What does holography have to do with anything?"

Dr. Principo explains his theory. "A hologram, when illuminated with lasers, can project a three-dimensional image in a dark room. As you know, the lighting in this room is dark except for the desk and floor lamps. You are looking at two-dimensional surfaces, but the images are precise three-dimensional images of real objects. You don't need special 3-D glasses to view them.

"You can view these images from different angles, as we did from our own seated positions in this room. The objects appear to move as you change your position. If you can cut an image in half, each half will contain the entire image, and even a small fragment will still contain the entire image.

"This is the part that Zachary has perfected. If you take a magnifying glass and make it a holographic image, it will magnify other objects in the hologram, just like a real glass would do. It is an image creating another image. It is my belief that he designed and built a miniature holographic projector, and installed it in the infrared focusing port on the video camera. He knew exactly where to place it in the room, where the bust of Sigmund Freud is now, so that it would be precisely centered over our heads. Since the recording part of the camera was also activated, he was able to project and record those flying books at the same time.

"It is also my belief that the so-called frequency generator and amplifier that he has in his pocket is really a miniature holographic projector. Has he made any objects change or morph, as he claims? Have you seen any evidence of this?"

"He made the video camera change into a toast rack and then made it disappear."

"Masterful, absolutely masterful, but now we know how he did it," Dr. Toussaint says. I'll wager if we ask to see the so-called electronic device in his pocket, he will not show it to us. The hand is quicker than the eye. It's easy to remove objects, especially if your victim is not expecting it."

"Is this all you have to report, Agent Krugman? It really isn't much to go on." Daphne is being protective of Zachary.

"At IBX he is in constant contact with several Scandinavian partner hospitals. One in Sweden and two in

Norway. It is entirely possible that he learned of Lars Pettersen's fortune through those contacts. We're now assessing just how much information about your inheritance was known outside the courts. I feel confident we can establish a link. It is my opinion, after talking with the doctors, that you are being gaslighted. Intent to defraud by doing psychological harm is a crime. I want him to know that he's being watched."

"Have you been in contact with my parents during this investigation?"

"I have."

"No wonder they were so intrusive. How dare you invade my privacy? What the hell did you say to them?"

"I explained that your husband was under investigation, and I suggested that they withhold any family funds from you until his name is cleared. It's for your own protection. We don't want to see you in possession of millions of dollars if your husband is intent on doing you harm. He is your beneficiary, is that not correct?"

"Of course he is, and our children. This is horrible. What you're saying to me is that as soon as my family money is transferred to me, I'm going to wind up at the bottom of the lake. You are completely mad. You're the ones who need a good psychiatrist. He's a loving husband and father."

"There is a lot of circumstantial evidence," Dr. Principo says. We don't want you to come to grief. If Zachary is innocent of wrongdoing, he is desperately in need of care, because he is *highly* delusional. There are other things. Small things, but they all add up. I noticed in one of our sessions, when I left the room to get some nut tarts, he had moved his chair three feet to the right. It was then directly under the light fixture. He's tall enough to easily stand on the chair, unscrew the glass, and install two-way communication devices. No, I didn't see him do it, but he could have."

The two doctors ask Daphne to recap what happened the previous week. She didn't go into much detail but hinted that she experienced the drug herself.

"Daphne, will you do something for us? It's for your own protection. Will you take a simple blood test? We would like to see if you have been given any mind-altering drugs, such as LSD. When drugs like these are combined with hypnosis and holograms, the results can be very dramatic. I guarantee what you were given was not PowZak. It doesn't exist. I know this is difficult, but there is greater danger in not knowing," Dr. Toussaint says.

"Like hell I will! If this is all you have to say, we've had our last session. I'm telling my husband that you set the FBI on him. You should be ashamed of yourselves." Daphne grabs her coat and briskly walks back to her car.

"I was afraid of this. She's been co-opted, and now either shares his delusions, or is in the terrible position of being a potential victim. She may or may not tell him about the FBI," Dr. Principo says. "However, I think Zachary can't afford *not* to keep his next appointment with us. He needs to know what we are up to for his own protection. I would like to see him alone this time. He's smart, all right, but I have the skill to pin him down. He's backed into a corner, and there are no more smoke and mirror tricks at his disposal."

"I'll go along with your treatment plan for the time being," Agent Krugman says. "However, if our investigation uncovers any links in Norway, our next session will be held at the FBI office in downtown Burlington. See if you can get Daphne to have those tests. Perhaps the parents can help convince her. There is something else I forgot to tell you. I requested information from *The Huffington Post*. Zachary did indeed send in the story and recording about the Tea Party congressman. We're not yet sure how he did it. He's as slick as owl shit."

«««◇»»»

"How's your Huckleberry doing, Em?" Daphne is tired but composed in front of her daughter.

"It's back to normal. I know Dad did it. I can tell."

"How can you tell? We have no proof. Why would he want to?"

245

"Because he hates it when I text my friends. He says it's a waste of time, and that I will not learn how to interact with real people. Hello, who does he think I'm interacting with?"

"He has a good point, Em. I've seen get-togethers of young people. Do you remember our last mother-daughter party? You kids sat there awkwardly without speaking. But as soon as you got your gadgets in your hands, you were all *so* animated. The electronic devices, including computers, are replacing person-to-person speech."

"Tell me that he wasn't responsible. Can you do that?"

"No, because I don't know."

"Now you're lying. You can't fool me, you know. You talk about respect. You can't demand respect from your daughter. I'm repeating what you have said to me: You can demand obedience, you can demand compliance, but not respect. Respect has to be earned. Why won't you answer me truthfully?"

"Because I don't honestly know. Your father is capable of many great, and probably not-so-great, things."

"What does he do all the time in his study? What's in that locked cabinet, and why is there now a lock on the outside door? You use locks for one reason only: to keep people away from something. Why does he need a huge padlock on a cabinet in his study, and why is he afraid of his own family?"

"You should ask *yourself* that question, young woman. Do you remember when you took his revolver and shot it in the basement to test hollow-point bullets? I know he keeps his gun in there. You want your privacy respected, so you should respect his."

"Is infecting the communication devices of my entire school respecting privacy?"

"That's enough, Em! You have no proof. Now let's talk about something else. How was basketball practice? You got in the game last week for the first time."

"Big deal. The coach has her favorite players, and they hate anyone else who tries to play because one of them has to sit down. I don't feel like I'm on a team. I feel like an outsider who has been shunned by a clique, and the coach is too blind to see what's happening. There are ten girls on the team, and only six get to play. They aren't even the best players. Mrs. Berkshire is a moron."

"Oh, I see what you mean. Why don't you quit?"

"Not a chance. By the time I'm finished, I intend to be the leading scorer."

"I worry about you, Em. You're too driven. You are much too intense for a girl of fourteen. I want to see you happy."

"My intensity makes me happy. I learned that from my parents." She sticks out her tongue at her mother. Daphne shakes her head and hugs Emma. "I've created a monster."

«««‹›»»»

The pin-and-tumbler lock consists of a cylinder that can rotate within its housing (see illustrations below). When the correct key is inserted, it pushes the pairs of pins. The cylinder can be turned and the lock will open.

Emma is using her computer and has found several sites on how to pick a padlock. She downloads plans to make a tension wrench and pick out of paperclips and a bobby pin. Emma makes a printout of the step-by-step instructions.

Apply light torque to the tension wrench in the correct direction, and hold. The required torque will vary from lock to lock and from pin to pin, so this may require some trial and error.

Use the pick to press the stubborn pin with just enough force to overcome the downward pressure of the spring. Your pick is pushing against the lower pin, which in turn pushes against the upper pin. Your goal is to push the upper pin completely out of the cylinder.

"Em, Ethan and I are going shopping. Do you want to come?"

"No thanks, Mom, I'll just stay here and waste all my time texting my no-good friends," Emma says as she quickly switches her computer screen.

"I can always count on you for a little drama."

"You can count on me for a lot of drama. Don't forget Eskimo Pies."

"You eat too many of those."

"Perhaps, but I burn them off. The refined sugar makes me hyper and difficult to deal with. Drive safely, the snow is deep."

Emma goes to work picking the lock to her father's study. It's a padlock with a half-inch shank. She uses her step-by-step instructions and easily opens it in less than two minutes. She enters the room, which is very tidy. The window shades are drawn, so she turns on the floor lamp. The lamp illuminates the locked cabinet. There is a large combination lock securely in place. *Shit, this won't work.* She noses around the desk but finds nothing of interest. Emma closes the door and relocks the padlock.

She goes back to her computer and researches how to pick a combination lock. Emma knows that there isn't enough time to do it before her mother and Ethan come home, but she does download all the information.

As you turn the dial clockwise with tension on the shackle, you will come to a point where you can't turn the dial anymore. Make note of where it stops. Sometimes it will stick to the right on the numbers, but sometimes it will be between the numbers.

Thank God for Wikipedia, Emma muses as she downloads detailed instructions. She needs the serial number off the lock, so she runs back to her father's study, picks the outside lock, and copies the number from the combination lock. Five minutes later, her mother arrives home.

"Peppermint Eskimo Pies!" Ethan is holding the frozen bars and teases Emma. "They are all mine and you can't have any."

"I don't want your peppermint Eskimo Pies, you little cretin. I like the dark chocolate."

"Stop fighting. Ethan, don't you dare use that word. Em, we also got the dark chocolate. You kids are going to be as fat as a hipporosahouros."

"What's that?" Ethan asks his mother.

"It's a huge animal that has two heads. All it does is eat from both ends. It does this for a long time until it finally explodes. So you'd better go easy on those pies."

Daphne can sense that Emma has been involved in something secretive. Her body language and glances are easily read.

"Em, don't even think of breaking into your father's study. You leave that gun alone."

"Don't worry, Mom, that was just a stage I was going through. I no longer care about ballistics. Now I'm into death stars, poison, and subliminal torture."

Daphne laughs and almost drops the carton of cage-free eggs. "Let me know what you learn. It may be useful in our school or in dealing with your father."

Zachary comes home from work and hugs everyone. "I picked up some Eskimo Pies. I noticed we were out of them." Daphne and the kids laugh and open the freezer. "Daphne, how was your session?"

She shakes her head no. He follows her into the bedroom. She is in tears, and she tells him that the doctors have called in the FBI and suspect he's a criminal who is after her family money. "They think you're trying to gaslight me and drive me crazy."

Chapter Nineteen

"Don't think badly of the doctors. There is no one as obsessed as a scientist whose empirical evidence has been challenged. They think the worst of me, but it makes absolutely no sense. They are clinicians of the mind, but they aren't capable of using simple logic. I'm angry that they upset you by calling in this Krugleman, or whatever the hell his name is."

"His name is Krugman, and he wants me to take a blood test to see if you've given me LSD or another mind-altering drug."

"Oh shit, they really are pulling out all the stops. Daphne, you should get the tests to keep them quiet. What else are they saying?"

"That you made the toast rack appear by using holograms. The electronic device you showed me is really not a signal generator and amplifier, but a miniature projector. You also used a projector when you made those books move in the doctor's office. You built it into the video recorder."

"Here it is, in my pocket. I've made two of them. One is in my study, and this is the other. I know you're not an electronics expert, but do you see any kind of projector? This knob controls the frequency, and this controls the strength of the current. Why would you need two electrodes for a projector? There are no lenses of any kind.

"Holograms? Holograms? Wait a minute. Dr. Principo and company are smarter than I thought. They must have found out that I often use the MIT library. Only the FBI can access that information. My colleague, Dr. Juan Aranjuez, and I are working on a presentation showing cellular structure. We are demonstrating the interaction of human cells with our new drug using three-dimensional holographic images. This is a legitimate IBX research project. The presentation will be made in front of top management and all the stockholders. Why don't you come to work with me, and I'll introduce you to him. He can explain what we're doing. If that FBI inquiry gets back to IBX, I will have some explaining to do. The bastards!

"Daphne, I don't want your family's money. I think it's great that you're rich, although I do feel less important financially. I don't give a rat's ass what your parents do with their money. Why don't you draft a post-nuptial agreement like we discussed? In the event of your death, all your family money reverts back to your parents' management. I'll sign it, and we can have it notarized."

"My mother will still suspect you and think it's some kind of trick."

"This is a no-win situation for me. Look, we're so spoiled. I switched from my 25-year-old Scotch to an 18-year-old. That's a big sacrifice? I don't care about money. I just want to have enough to enjoy our lifestyle, which is highly extravagant by any world standards. I want to paddle my canoe on the lake, make love to you, be able to send the kids to college, and take a nice vacation every year. By the way, we are *way* overdue for one.

"The doctors are mistaking my reluctance to share the specifics of my PowZak discovery as a sign that something else is going on, because they know I'm not delusional. I'm going to turn the whole project over to Cornell University. When I show them my research notes, documentation of my experiments, and specific instructions on how to replicate what I've done, it will end this nightmare once and for all. I will stipulate a condition that none of the research be shared with the U.S. government or any military organization. I've had it with all the intrigues and am very unhappy for the pain it has caused you. All I want now is to be rid of it."

"Oh no, you're not! That formula stays right here. Don't you dare give it to anyone! The doctors are out of the picture as of right now, and so is Cornell. As of today, this is a family research project, and I'm your partner. The kids are waiting for us, and we have to make dinner."

«‹‹‹‹›››»

Emma has come home directly after her last class. She has one hour before her mother arrives with Ethan. She picks the padlock on the door to her father's study and notices that the floor lamp is lit. *Holy shit, I forgot to turn off the lamp. I wonder if he used his study last night.*

She follows the instructions to open the combination lock.

Determine the sticking point by finding the number that's in the midpoint of the sticking range. A range of 4 and 5 would have a sticking point of 4.5. A range of 22.5 and 23.5 would have a sticking point of 23.

"Wikipedia is right again," she says out load as she snaps open the lock. The cabinet is empty except for two sweaters folded neatly on the top shelf. There is a note tacked to the middle shelf.

Thou shalt not snoop in thy father's private cabinet, or he will turn you into a toad. I love you anyway.

"You think you're so smart!" Emma is very angry. "I know you wrote those messages, and I'm going to find out how."

She stares at his library and examines it closely. There is a fine layer of dust on the shelves except for three places where

255

books have been taken out. One of them is a book on theology. *He's not interested in theology.* Her instincts tell her to examine it. She opens the front cover and finds that the two-inch-thick volume is actually a book safe. She lifts up the felt-covered door and finds a small electronic device and an atomizer. There is a chart with a scale from one to fifty, with some kind of multiples alongside each number. There is a third column with a frequency and milliamp setting for each dose. There is a red line after twenty with a warning. "Do not exceed twenty doses unless compound A is available as an antidote."

What is this stuff?

《《《〈〉》》》

Emma is sitting on her deck. It's a nice sunny day, and her neighbor's cat, Jethro, walks tentatively towards her. He puffs his tail and arches his back. He walks alongside the house, where the overhang has kept the snow away. There is a one-foot-wide path for him to pass. Emma is sitting on the arm of one of the dark cedar Adirondack chairs that Zachary had brought out to talk with Daphne. The sun has warmed the surface, and it's free of snow. Jethro jumps onto the seat.

"What's wrong with you, Jethro? Why are you puffing your tail?"

"I've never seen you before," Jethro replies. "How do you know my name? Do you live around here?"

"Oh, my God!" Emma is excited. "The cat talked. I heard the cat talk. I shouldn't have taken the highest dose of that drug. Now I'm hearing things."

"Of course I can talk. Humans only hear *meow*, but you and I know we have a language. Didn't your parents teach you anything? Why, you're just out of kittenhood. Have you had any litters yet?"

"No, I haven't met the right Tom," Emma coyly replies.

"I don't want to talk about it," Jethro says, yowling and hissing. "I'm very upset. How would humans feel if their balls were cut off? I can't be your Tom, because I'm neutered. Humans are spaying and neutering every cat they find. What a bunch of hypocrites. All the conservatives are against eugenics and stem cell research. The idea of interfering in human reproduction is scary to them. Yet these same people are taking away our sexuality. Did it ever occur to these morons that there will be no more alley cats? All that will be left will be purebred Siamese, Burmese, Persian, and other high-strung felines who are as useless as shit. All they can do is sit on fluffy cushions looking pretty. They couldn't kill a rat if they had to. They would starve first.

"Have you met the cats who live two doors down? Their names are Boris and Natasha, both seal-point Siamese. They don't let them out, so we have to speak through the sliding glass door. They aren't of show quality, so they have also been neutered. I feel like sharpening my claws on their jailor's private parts."

Jethro puts his nose close to Emma's tail. "You smell great. I can tell that they haven't gotten to you yet."

"Don't get too familiar, we just met." She cuffs him with her right paw, but with her claws retracted.

"Jethro, Jethro, here kitty."

"Gotta go, time for Newman's Own beef and liver. You ought to try that. Claw their favorite furniture every time they give you cat tuna. That tastes disgusting. Those fish dinners should be fed to dogs. See you around, Tabby."

"Emma, the name's Emma."

Cats have been on Emma's mind ever since she and her friends wrote a one-act play. They dressed up as felines and staged the production on a set that looked like a backyard fence. When she saw Jethro, she morphed into that life form. Unfortunately, she shut the door behind her when she stepped out onto the deck. She tries to jump for the doorknob. She can reach it, but not turn it at the same time.

Shit, I'm stuck here until Mom gets home.

"Em, Em, we're home. Ethan, tell Em that I found that photography book at the library."

"Can't find her, Mom, but there's a cat meowing at the back door."

Daphne opens the door and the cat, a tortoiseshell tabby, scoots in before she can block her path. She runs into the kitchen, jumps onto the table, and meows mournfully.

"Poor kitty must be hungry," Ethan says, petting Emma. She purrs loudly.

"If we feed her, Ethan, she will never go away. She does look like she's in great shape, a very pretty kitty. Okay, we'll give her some tuna. Em must be at Carol's house working on their play. I wish she'd leave me a note."

Emma is frightened. She knows she has to wait for her father to come home and somehow show him what happened. She doesn't know how to change back into a human. When her mother sits on the couch, she crawls onto her lap and falls asleep.

«««‹›»»»

"Daphne got her blood test, and I'm having the results analyzed by special request. The hospital lab routines are all the same. They check for diseases and the presence of the usual drug types. I told them I wanted to know every chemical compound that is found. I want a complete analysis. As you know, we all have traces of things like mercury, lead, arsenic, and other harmful substances in our blood. I want to know everything, so I got the medical lab at UVM involved. We should hear something in a day or two."

Dr. Principo is on the phone with Dr. Toussaint. "Ill bet they find LSD or a similar drug. There's no doubt in my mind. I'm surprised that Daphne agreed to have it done. Pierre? Pierre? Are you still there?" There is temporary silence at the other end.

"Antonio, the only reason why she agreed is because Zachary told her she should get it done. That means we will *not* find any drugs in her system. That son of a bitch is one step ahead of us, as usual."

"Not find any? I don't see how that's possible. Let's wait for the results."

«««<>»»»

"Hello Daphne, hello little buddy. Oh goody, *Ratatouille* arrived from NetFlix. We should watch that tonight. What a cute kitty. Where did she come from? Where's Em?"

Emma meows loudly, runs down the hall, and stands in front of her father's study, scratching at the door. Daphne remains in the kitchen. The microwave will go off in thirty seconds, and she will reach for the tea she has warmed.

"That's odd." Zachery opens the padlock and the cat runs to his bookcase. She jumps on the third shelf, balancing precariously on the edge as only a cat can do. She takes her paw and pokes at the book safe with the PowZak inside.

"Em, if that is you, lift your left paw in the air three times, and then your right paw twice." Emma does as instructed.

"You little monster, I should leave you as a cat and feed you rancid kitty tuna for the rest of your life. Cats can't use Huckleberries, you know. Mouse catcher would be your only occupation. What do you think of that, young lady?"

Emma hisses and puffs up her tail.

Zachary puts seven drops of compound A antidote in a teaspoon. "Here, lick this. Now concentrate on being Em. You will no longer be a cat."

Emma is now herself. Daphne walks into the study with the cup of tea she has brewed. She looks at her daughter just as she morphs from being a cat, gasps, and drops the tea on the rug.

"Meow," Emma says as she hugs her mom. "I'm glad I'm back to being a human. I didn't want to wind up spayed and wearing a flea collar."

«««‹›»»»

"No, Mother, it is you who will cease and desist. You will quit interfering in my life. I'm not in any danger, and

261

Zachary has discovered something that will change the world."

"Oh, I'm sure he has you brainwashed into thinking he has. We will not support you with him. By the way, thanks for the nut tarts."

"You're welcome. Here we go again with your threats of withholding the family fortune. Do you know what is going to happen if you continue down this road? We will not visit you, and you will have no contact with your only grandchildren. Your financial blackmail will backfire in your faces. I promise you this. In spite of your making Zachary your enemy, he continues to be patient and understanding. It's a miracle he hasn't thrown a temper tantrum and cut you off entirely."

"Cut *us* off?"

"Yes, Mother. There's more to life than money. If you lose his affection, you will be very much the poorer. I don't know why you are talking with the FBI, but you are one inch away from losing your family. Do I make myself clear?"

"Did you have those blood tests that Dr. Principo requested? You have your children to consider, and you are blind to Zachary's manipulation. He must have you hypnotized and brainwashed."

"Goodbye, Mother."

"We've got the tests back." The two doctors are sitting in the study. They both sit in chairs at the front of the desk and are passing papers back and forth.

"Here's a list of the compounds they found in Daphne. There are the usual traces of aspirin, lead, probably from her childhood days breathing lead-laced car fumes. Here are two mystery compounds that we must research. They did isolate two drugs that were found in much higher quantities than any others, doxazene and methylthiazide. I'm not familiar with either of them, so I've contacted the chemistry department for their take. I don't know what will happen when they are combined." Dr. Principo hands the printout to his colleague.

Dr. Toussaint hands another printout to his friend. "Look what it says on that sheet. There is another compound that is unknown. It consists of two or more chemicals that have been combined. It will take further analysis to separate them. It may not be possible to isolate the individual elements, and we may have to analyze it as a combined substance. I wonder what the relationship is with the other two. They were all taken at the same time, and very recently. I believe we may have found our hallucinogen."

"Pierre, I'm going to ask the researchers at UVM to make up this compound and test it on rats. Perhaps we can see if they are mind altering. "

263

Dr. Toussaint shrugs. "But who knows what's in a rat's mind? This research will take time. Can we get them to speed it up?"

"We can if we get the FBI involved. Let's do it. I guess Zachary didn't count on our using advanced analysis. However, I feel uneasy. He usually doesn't miss anything. He must want us to find these compounds, possibly as proof of his drug's existence."

«««‹›»»»

Emma gobbles up two Eskimo Pies with reckless abandon. She is sitting at the kitchen table with her parents. They don't lecture her about eating too many sweets, because she has had the most traumatic experience of her young life.

"Thank you for not saying anything. Of course, I know what you wanted to say about junk food. Did you ever hear the Redd Foxx line? 'Those health food nuts are going to feel pretty stupid someday, lying in hospitals dying of nothing.'

"The food tastes so good. My senses of smell and hearing are incredible. Ethan is asleep in his room, and I can hear him breathing. I never could before. Will this last?"

"For about a week," her father replies. "All your senses will be heightened, and you will have abilities that you don't normally have. You must be very careful not to do anything in public that people might find shocking. Try to be in the background for the next week."

"But I have a basketball game tomorrow night."

"I suggest that you don't play. You don't know how to control your strength when you are in this heightened condition."

"So this is what's been going on around here. I can understand why you didn't tell me about it. I really liked being a cat. I wish I could change back again. Jethro is kind of cute, poor thing. I'm sorry I scared youse guys. That stuff is otherworldly. What are we going to do with it? Does anyone else know about it?"

"Two shrinks do, but they don't believe the results and think you father is nuts, or that he wants to drive me crazy to get your grandparents' money."

"God, life is complicated. I feel really weird. Like I can never go back to the way things were."

"You have to put it out of your mind, Em." Zachary is insistent.

"Yeah, right. I have the highest IQ in the school, you have opened Pandora's box with the secret of the universe, and you tell me to put it out of my mind. Great, I will, just as soon as the two of you put it out of yours."

«««‹›»»»

265

Collins has come out of the game and Emma Warren is in at forward. There's five minutes left in the first half, and the other team, CVU, leads by nine points. The Warren family is sitting on the wooden bleachers. Ethan shouts Yay! when his sister is put into the game.

Zachary whispers to Daphne. "This is against my better judgment. She reassured us that she won't do anything outrageous, but how can she help it? She's dramatic and wants to impress the coach and her teammates. This is a recipe for disaster. I almost can't look."

Emma is holding up both arms as she defends the outside in a one, two, two zone. She suddenly sprints between two offensive players and intercepts their pass. She runs the length of the court, does a 360-degree spin, and slam dunks the basketball. She bends the rim down, and it snaps back into position. On the next play, she leaps high in the air to block a shot, scooping it high off the backboard. At the other end, she takes a pass from her teammate and does a reverse stuff, again bending the rim downward. The CVU coach calls a time out. Ethan and Daphne are stamping their feet on the wooden stands, and pandemonium erupts in the bleachers. Zachary has his hand over his eyes.

Chapter Twenty

"Here are the results of the lab tests. They needed a total of nine days to get preliminary data. It took one day to combine doxazene and methylthiazide in the exact proportions found in Daphne. They injected the rats, and this is what happened."

Principo reads the report to Toussant.

Four white laboratory rats were injected with the doxazene-methylthiazide compound, placed in a large enclosure with four rats free of this substance, and their behavior contrasted for three days. All observations indicate complete detachment of the drug-injected rats from the other rats. When one drugged rat initiated any type of behavior, the other rats that had been administered the drug would follow. They all seem to have the ability to lead in this manner.

They repeated none of their previous routines. Changes to their behavior patterns were observed as follows:

- The rats that took the drug would lie on their backs and kick all four legs in the air.
- They would copulate indiscriminately with members of both sexes.
- They would run around in circles chasing their tails.
- They would climb up the side of the cage and do backwards flips and triple somersaults.
- They would vocalize in strange squeaks and chirps and repeat the sounds over again as if they were communicating with each other.
- They figured out how to open the combination lock securing their inner cage, and were studying ways of opening the heavy outer latch. It took a large padlock to keep the cage secured.

The rats that were not given the drug exhibited normal behavior. The early indication is that these drugs are indeed mind-altering to a high degree. It will take further study to determine the extent of the changes.

Days four through six showed a decrease in aberrant behavior, presumably as the effects of the drug wore off. No neurological or physical damage or side effects were observed on day six. By day nine, they were back to normal. They were re-tested for damage and side effects and none were found.

"Here are the results of a computer simulation by Dr. Silas McCann, who is a neurological expert at UVM Medical School, and Dr. Caroline Brown, who is an expert in cognitive behavior patterns."

Our projections indicate that if a human took this drug, his/her sensory perceptions would be entirely sealed off from reality. She/he would exist only in the world his/her mind created, to the exclusion of all other data. Unlike other hallucinogens, these drugs cause the subject to suffer a complete detachment from reality and the environment around them.

Since the laboratory rats were observed to follow the lead of other rats that were also in this state, it would seem that the drug-induced reality can only be shared by those subjects who have also taken the drug. The drugged rats did not acknowledge the presence of or interact with the four rats in the control group, and worked as a team to open the combination lock. How they did that is still a mystery, although it was possibly a random event.

The human subject who takes this drug will be highly suggestible to his/her own imagination, and to the imaginations of others who have taken the drug, but not to any other outside stimulus. All events occurring outside the human subject's drug-induced perceptions will be filtered through an unreality filter that the drug will create.

"Pierre, they said that the other compound will take a while to analyze. The trace amounts of one element could be silphocane. This is another chemical that seems to be a variant of an amphetamine."

"Let me sum it up as I see it, Antonio. Zachary has not lied to us. When the effects of this drug have worn off, he believes that everything he has fantasized about is real. Only to him, it isn't fantasy. It has become part of his psyche. He has constructed elaborate protective defense mechanisms that are as real to him as eating and sleeping. I'm sorry to say that I don't see any way it can be purged from his mind, and I fear that Daphne has also acquired permanent delusions. God forbid if their daughter has taken any. If this drug ever gets out on the street, it could cause a societal collapse."

"I agree with you. It has taken over the Warren family, people of the highest intelligence and discipline, who have everything to lose. I doubt anyone could use it as one might marijuana, with a take-it-or-leave-it attitude. This experiment with rats reminds me of another. In that experiment, the rats could administer a drug to themselves by pressing a lever. There were no controls or limits to the amount of heroin, I believe it was, they could use. They kept using it until they died from the overdoses."

Dr. Principo continues, "The manufacture and distribution of this drug must be prevented by any and every means possible. The government has the right to regulate any controlled substance that is harmful to the populace. This isn't a patient's rights issue, it is a federal issue.

"Zachary did not keep his last two appointments because he is angry with us. I'm going to attempt to get him to give us his data. My intuition is that now he and Daphne are excluding all others when they take this drug. Don't forget for one minute that he truly believes he has discovered something wonderful that will save mankind. If we fail to get him to present all his data, I'm going to call agent Krugman and recommend that all Zachary's records and lab results be confiscated with a surprise search warrant. I had no idea when we agreed to treat this man for a suspected delusional disorder that we would uncover a sinister health threat of titanic proportions. Perhaps it's lucky that we did, for everyone's sake. The seriousness of this situation completely overrides doctor-patient privacy issues."

"Antonio, clinicians like us have always tried to be direct and honest with those patients who suffer from delusional disorder. A patient's right to privacy and the confidentiality of his treatment is usually sacred above all else but, I agree, not in this case. I feel terrible that we may have to sacrifice Dr. Zachary Warren and Daphne for a so-called greater good. Perhaps he will agree to hypnosis. I have no faith that it will work, but we are rapidly running out of ideas. When the last compound is analyzed, it is also possible we can discover an antidote that will purge the delusions from his system, sort of like using lime to neutralize acid. Why don't you call him this evening and see if he will agree to see us?"

"I will, but there is something else that concerns me. I read in the paper last week that Emma Warren, their daughter, scored thirty five points in her basketball game. She made sports headlines in *The Burlington Free Press*."

"I don't know much about the game, is this a big achievement?"

"No, but I'll tell you what is. She's only a fourteen-year-old girl, who is five-foot-seven. Yet she was able to do a complete spin in the air and slam-dunk a basketball through a rim ten feet high. There has never been a recorded incident of a middle, high school, or college girl accomplishing a slam dunk in the entire state of Vermont. Not ever. What does this mean? Pierre, people can accomplish amazing things when they are in an altered state. They can mobilize and channel their resources, and perfectly distribute controlled energy to every muscle. It scares me to question how she was able to accomplish this amazing athletic feat. Is there a coincidence here? I must talk to her father.

"It will be a very long while before enough is known about PowZak, as he calls it, before it can be tested on human subjects, if it ever can be. Primate testing will probably be the first order. Perhaps in some prison, a death row inmate who has nothing to lose would agree, perhaps for a pardon. We have discovered a new disease, a delusional addiction. This is an awful mess, Pierre. This is an awful mess."

«««◇»»»

"Hello Em, how do you feel today?

"I feel absolutely great. Could we adopt a few kitties? I will make it my job to take care of them."

"I was wondering when you would ask," Daphne says. "The answer is a definite yes, as long as you don't try to join them and stand on the back fence meowing at three in the morning."

"Can't we find some strays, or answer ads in the newspaper for kittens? I don't want an altered cat from the animal shelter."

"Sure, but remember, Em, if we adopt a female, and she has kittens, we can't keep them all and will have to put them up for adoption. You will have no control over whether or not they will be altered or spayed. You are flying in the face of all animal control logic, and no one in the community will support your viewpoint."

"That's a good caution, Mom, and I will agree to put them up for adoption."

"Are you sure you want to do that Em?" her father asks. "You could be involved in much more worthy pursuits."

Both Daphne and Emma sense that he is about to say something provocative and probably very funny, so they listen intently.

"Did you know that Ohio native Andrew Acklin has set the world record for most text messages sent or received in a single month? He sent a total of 200,052. He has been acknowledged by both the World Records Academy, and the Universal Records Database. Now *there's* something that you should do, Em. Are you going to let a man from Ohio send and receive more text messages than you do? Where is your competitive spirit? You could use two Huckleberries at the same time, one in each hand. We will support your staying home from school. You can text day and night, rain or shine, from the kitchen while eating, from the bathroom, and from the car. You can ignore your family and the entire world around you. Surely that must appeal?"

"Dad, when you were little, did anyone ever beat you up?"

"No, I beat up everyone else, especially mouthy women and fourteen-year-old girls. Why?"

"Just wondering."

Daphne sneaks behind Zachary, pulls back the collar of his shirt, and squirts cold whipped cream down his back. He jumps straight up out of his chair. "OOO, very cold."

Zachary goes into the bedroom to change, and Daphne follows him. "The good doctors called while you all were out shopping. They want to see us again on our terms. Agent Krugman will not be there. Dr. Principo acknowledged that they have been wrong about their diagnosis and treatment.

They want to discuss a transfer of information about our discovery."

"No good, Zachary. They are telling you what you want to hear. They've obviously found something in the lab tests, as we knew they would. What guarantees do we have that they won't confiscate the formula with the help of the FBI? I get distinct indications that that is their intent."

"You may be correct, Daphne. If the FBI could confiscate our computers because they suspected terrorism, they can also burst into our home with or without a search warrant and look for PowZak. I'm going to remove everything from my hard drives and take all physical evidence, formulas, electronics, everything, out of the house. If they make a surprise visit, they will find nothing, and I will complain to our senator."

«««‹›»»»

"Why don't the two of you want to share your information? If your drug does as you claim, surely you want to make it available for further research." Dr. Toussaint is no longer talking to Zachary as a patient who needs therapy. His hidden agenda is treating a delusional addict who must be stripped of his creation.

"We've been through this before. I don't want it to fall into the wrong hands. You may deny it, but both Daphne and I are completely certain that you have a contingency plan in place to send in the FBI if we refuse to hand over our

275

information. I can assure you that they will find nothing, so please save us the cleanup and keep them away.

"Daphne and I disagree on how to proceed from here. I want to turn over all my research to Cornell University, with a stipulation that no government or military types may have access to the data."

"And I disagree, because I don't want anyone to get their hands on it. It's too powerful. I want to keep it in the family."

"Zachary, Daphne, I do not want to make either of you uncomfortable or afraid of what we might do. I will confess, right here and now, that there are so many unknowns in this case, it makes our heads spin. My honest belief is...well, let me give you a little background. Hypnotherapy is used for many things, and no, I'm not any longer suggesting that either of you be hypnotized. It's used for everything from treating phobias and anxiety, to pain management, post traumatic stress disorder, athletic and academic performance, and a host of other things. I truly believe that you have hypnotized yourselves, using a combination of a hallucinogen and suggestions from each other's imaginations.

"As a result of your blood test, which you were kind enough to provide, Daphne, they isolated chemicals that are highly hallucinogenic. Lab tests have confirmed this. The fantasies you have created have stayed with you as reality in your psyches, as though the events had actually happened.

You have constructed elaborate scientific explanations and support, and truly believe that you have invented a wonder drug that will change the world. We're waiting for the results of more lab tests. There is a possibility that we may be able to create an antidote."

"I have already created an antidote called compound A."

"I know you think you have, Zachary, but my challenge to you now is the same as the challenge I verbalized when we first talked about PowZak. I don't want to see projected holograms of books flying through the air. Dr. Toussaint and I want to set up our own camera and record you giving us a concrete example of the drug's power that we can document."

"And show to whom? If we do show you further proof that the drug exists, how will that alter your opinion and actions?" Daphne asks.

"Good question," Dr. Toussaint says. "We have not allowed for the possibility that you *can* offer any real proof. I suppose if we were confronted with the unexpected and unexplained evidence that PowZak does what you say it can do, I personally would have to suggest that it be locked away for good from the general public, the government, and the military. I would agree that a secure university research setting would be most proper."

"That's an interesting viewpoint, Doctor, but I believe it's somewhat naïve. The FBI already knows about our meetings, and no doubt you have had separate sessions with them. How long do you think it would be before Cornell University would be raided, the data stolen, and placed under government control? It wouldn't take one week. That's why I disagree with Zachary."

"Before I forget, thanks for the nut tarts, Daphne. What do you put in them, besides the Amaretto liquor? They are most enjoyable."

"Almonds instead of walnuts."

"Almonds, so that's your secret! You have improved my original recipe. Please think long and hard about giving us some additional proof. Let us know when you have decided. I promise there will be no interference from the FBI."

Daphne and Zachary stand up and shake hands with the doctors. "Friday, at 12 noon, but no camera. I don't want to risk having a photographic record that could fall into the wrong hands. This is for your eyes only," Zachary says forcefully. "As I told you earlier, you'd better have something strong to drink to wash down those nut tarts."

«««◇»»»

The drive home from the Principo's office was filled with merriment and music. Daphne pulled out Zachary's classical guitar music from the car's CD player, put in the Rolling Stones, and turned up the volume. "You can't catch me, Oh baby, you can't catch me." They were both loudly singing along with their favorite Brit group.

"They are such cool guys. I hope I'm like that when I'm their age. You know, Daffy, I so much prefer morphing into animals over being a human. No offense intended, of course. Especially when I'm a hawk or a seagull, I want to soar above the Earth forever. I'm not at all convinced that we are the highest species on the planet. Far from it. If there is one thing I have learned from my experiments with PowZak, it is that everything alive has a consciousness of itself. Even inanimate objects have a presence that truly speaks to us, if we will only listen."

"That's what I want to do next, fly," Daphne says as she puts her head on her husband's shoulder.

"Mom, Dad, I didn't do the right thing." Her parents have taken off their coats and hung them in the mudroom. Em is whimpering. "It's Ethan. He's floating in the air."

They all run into Ethan's bedroom, and sure enough, he is gently rocking back and forth, suspended five feet above his bed. He is humming a Brahms lullaby.

"Em, what the hell did you do?" Zachary is angry but is not raising his voice.

"Before you took all the PowZak out of the house, I found where you hid it and squirted some into a paper cup. I took some this morning, just a little bit, honest, because I wanted to do real well in the game tomorrow. There must have been some left in the cup, and Ethan drank water out of it. I'm so sorry. Will he be all right?"

Chapter Twenty One

Every once in a rare while, a perfect winter day presents itself in the North Country. Today, January 23rd, the date of Zachary's birth, is just such a day. The temperature is twenty-five degrees, there isn't a cloud in the sky, there is no wind, and the sun is reflecting off the recent snowfall that has covered the ground and all the tree branches. Except near the shore, where the water has turned to ice, Lake Champlain is open. Cormorants, seagulls, terns, and an occasional osprey can be seen fishing in the shallows.

"I'm sorry we had that misunderstanding, Daphne, and I'm glad that you and Zachary are seeing Dr. Principo again. He's such a good and capable man. I think Dr. Toussaint is cute. Oh goody, more nut tarts. I really like these. Why doesn't your husband come with you on these visits? I have a birthday present for him."

"Do you really want me to answer that question?"

"Will you give him the present for me?"

"No, I will not. It will do both of you good if you hand it to him yourself. Where's Dad?"

"He's visiting his friend John in Brattleboro and spent the night. He won't be home until two."

"I can't stay long, Mom. As a matter of fact, we have an appointment with both doctors at twelve. We'll see you later on this afternoon."

"We'll be by before dark. Your father and I have been invited out to dinner by the school superintendent. We're being courted, for some reason. Couldn't be our newfound wealth, now could it?"

"Now you're learning, Mom. You are not going to believe how many new friends you are going to make. How many politicians have contacted you?"

"Them I expect, but we've also received invitations from seven local churches. I didn't know that extreme wealth made you holier. Perhaps it's just the opposite, and we need special guidance. I'm sure our big, fat tithe has nothing to do with all the attention."

"As I said, you are learning. All the more reason to respect those, ahem, those who stand their ground in spite of financial threats. See you later."

"Come in. So this is the big day. More nut tarts, thank you, thank you," Dr. Principo is animated and jovial, but Dr. Toussaint is dour, as usual. "Happy birthday Zachary. Daphne, I spoke with your mother last night. She is a tiger, and a real force of nature. I'm not trying to pry, but was it difficult growing up?"

"She's a pain in the ass, Zachary says."

That comment gets a rare chuckle out of Dr. Toussaint, who reaches for a nut tart. "We decided not to wash down your food with anything stronger than a cup of coffee. Would either of you care for any?"

"Sure," Zachary says, but Daphne politely declines.

There is a more than subtle undercurrent of tension in the room. The two doctors are puzzled by the calm, rational people who sit before them. The doctors are projecting more agida, as the Italians call it, than their patients. Daphne senses their unease and makes eye contact with Zachary. He understands her meaning and improvises on the spot.

"This is what I suggest. We will show you what PowZak can do. I believe it's best to tell you beforehand exactly what to expect. That way, there will be no shocking surprises. If we scientifically describe the physical changes that you will see, I'm hoping you can study them in the spirit of examining extraordinary evidence. We don't want to give anyone a heart attack.

"We are talking about *physical* changes here. I've used words like *morphing* and *changelings* to describe what happens. What you will observe is the outside manifestation that is caused by the drug's internal effects on the whole being. What is actually causing the change is highly involved and will take you much study. I'll describe the first thing that I'm going to do. Daphne will be observing this change along with the two of you. I'm going to keep my exact physical appearance. However, I'm going to shrink myself so that I'm only one foot tall. I'm going to do that now."

First he takes a paperclip and bends it slightly. He shows it to the doctors before placing it on the arm of his chair. During a time period of exactly ten seconds, done more slowly than usual so he doesn't shock the doctors, Zachary shrinks into a miniature version of himself. His voice is now much reduced in intensity, and he has to shout to be heard. He grabs the paperclip and uses both hands to hold it, much in the same way that an average person would grab a rolling pin.

"The next thing I'm going to do is morph into a chickadee and fly around the room. I will then land on the left arm of the chair that I am now sitting, excuse me, standing on, and then morph back into myself."

The doctors and Daphne observe him change, instantly this time, into a black-capped chickadee. He flies around the room, but before he lands on the arm of the chair, he flies over to the tray of nut tarts and takes a tiny bite out of one. He flies back onto the chair and turns back into himself. At first he was purely a form of light, a luminous human shape, but then all his features quickly come into focus.

"Mmm, those tarts are good. I love the almonds. This is the same paperclip." Zachary reaches onto the arm of the chair and grabs the object between his thumb and index finger. "That was not some special effect that Daphne produced by using a trick camera hidden in her shoe. This is the same clip that I was holding when I was a miniature version of myself."

The two doctors sit in stone silence and are quite pale.

"The next thing Daphne and I are going to do is turn ourselves into objects. We've chosen metallic objects. I want you to pick us up and examine us closely. You will see no difference between the objects we change into and any other similar object. We have chosen two silver dollars. Actually, two antique Morgan coins. She chose the year 1878, the first minted year, and I chose 1921, the last minted year. Please bear in mind that we can communicate with each other while we are in this shape. If you attempted to lock us in a drawer, or hit us with a hammer, it would have no effect. We can instantly change back to our original shape with a simple thought, and can combine our molecules with any other surface or object to repel threats. I'll show you more about that in a minute. Now the change."

The Warrens are now two shiny coins sitting on the arms of their chairs. Dr. Toussant grabs Daphne and holds her up to the light. Dr. Principo grabs Zachary, balancing him on his finger, while he strikes the edge with a pen to make a pleasant bell-like sound. After they morph back into themselves, Zachary is about to continue with their presentation, but Daphne stops him.

"Dear, I believe we have shown them quite enough for now. Remember this is quite shocking and is new to them. I'm sure you can show them the rest of what you have planned the next time we meet."

"Dr. Principo, what do you have to say about what you have seen?" Zachary asks.

"Actually, I have no comment at this time. I'm quite shaken and impressed, that's for sure, but I'm not certain what I just witnessed."

"How about you, Dr. Toussaint?"

"Masterful, absolutely masterful. There will be no next time, Dr. Zachary Warren, unless we can photograph the session. A third-party photographer will do the recording. When we have after-the-fact tangible empirical proof, we can act and plan accordingly. I will say that you have earned the right to that session, that's for sure. Amazing, absolutely amazing. You are probably the most brilliant illusionist couple who have ever lived."

"I'm not willing to accept that condition, good doctors. You have been shown ample and graphic proof. I can see that from now on the burden is on us. I assure you we can neutralize any attempts by the FBI to interfere. We have committed no crime, and they will find no proof. That leaves the next move up to myself and Daphne. We have decided not to turn the project over to Cornell University. It wouldn't take the government or corporate outsiders long to seize the data. We very much thank you for being an active part of our decision-making process. We can use your therapeutic guidance to help us cope with our discovery."

"Before you leave, let me assure you that there will be no interference from the FBI or from any other group that will invade your privacy. We will not betray your confidence, and I apologize for suspecting you of criminal intent. What you say in this office, stays in this office. I look forward to seeing both of you next week." Dr. Principo shakes both their hands.

The Warrens leave, and the two men recap what they have seen.

"Antonio, you know how I feel about these shenanigans, so don't ask. The obfuscation is multi-layered. They could be working as an advanced, highly-skilled illusionist team for the sole purpose of masking their intent to develop this drug."

"Then why did they contact us in the first place?"

"Because Daphne had not yet been brought into his world, and earlier on Zachary needed a cover. I'll wager that those other drugs that were found in Daphne are inert ingredients. He probably put those trace elements in to confuse whoever it was who would be doing the analysis. He's that smart, you know."

"Possible, Pierre, possible, but unlikely. Zachary is not a grand manipulator. He's much too direct. He isn't capable of Machiavellian intrigues. I do agree with you that he has developed an advanced hallucinogen. But because of additional evidence, such as the daughter Emma's incredible athletic performance, his own reaction time, which I personally tested, by the way, and other physical manifestations, such as his great strength lifting weights, his PowZak is more than a mind-altering substance. Somehow it effects the body as well. We both know that there's a mind-body connection. They have convinced themselves that if they can think it, they can be it. This is an interesting philosophical concept.

"There is no doubt in my mind that this drug can cause metabolic changes, possibly extreme changes. I strongly hope that you are right about illusions. If what we just witnessed isn't an illusion, the genie is truly out of the bottle, and we're going to need good therapists ourselves.

"I didn't have time to tell you, or to go into any details, but Agent Krugman said they couldn't find a Norwegian link that would have let Zachary know about his wife's family finances. The holographic research that he did at MIT was for a legitimate IBX project. He has committed no crime, and the FBI is officially off the case. I'm glad. I felt like a rat."

"What rats? We didn't know what his intent was. Antonio, this drug is still dangerous, although I agree with you that Zachary and Daphne aren't a threat to society. They will probably keep it for their own use; at least I hope so. It's good that you will continue an ongoing dialogue with them. Let me know if I can be of any help in the future.

"I'm glad that my family and I have reconciled." Dr. Toussaint shows a rare, genuine smile. "I wonder how Zachary learned about our *patching things up*, as he called it?"

"Pierre, I never said a word."

《《《《《◇》》》》

"Come on, slowpoke. Dad, he's always lagging behind."

"Em, be kind, he's not as fast as you are."

The Warren family is getting some exercise. They asked Zachary what he wanted to do on his birthday, and he said they should all take advantage of the beautiful winter afternoon.

"Daphne, how do you think the Sidtherns are doing? I'll bet they take a vacation to Saint Lucia. We should also go there. When they are elsewhere, of course."

"Those are the therapists who gave you that funny sex video, aren't they? I'll bet you don't see *them* anymore. Is this just for the two of you, or is it a family trip?" Emma asks her parents.

"A family trip, of course. We can go during spring break. It will be great to walk along those beaches after gliding low above the tree canopy."

Zachary turns his head around to look at his daughter. "Em, do you notice how much easier it is to fly when someone else is out in front to cut through the wind? It's like bicycle or auto racers who draft each other. The lead guy is doing all the work, while the others get in line behind him. When the timing is right, they break away to take the lead. There is great strategy involved. That's what geese do when they are in a V formation flying south. They take turns being in the lead. The reason why Ethan is last, is because he is the littlest and needs the least air resistance."

"He's a pain in the butt who always gets his own way."

"Language, Em."

"Dildo!"

"Ethan, I told you I never wanted to hear that word again. No television for you this weekend. You are being punished. Every time you use that word, the result will be the same. Is that clear?" Daphne has warned him before.

"She called me a pain in the butt, so why doesn't she get punished?"

The family has been circling the neighborhood and lands in the open water on Lake Champlain, at the edge of the ice.

"Mom, she's doing it again."

"What is it now, little buddy?" Zachary asks, losing patience.

"Every time I try to catch a minnow, she pushes me out of the way and steals it. This is *my* space. Tell her to sit somewhere else. Mom, my bottom is cold."

"Those fish are for everyone to eat, Ethan. They do not have your name on them. Don't worry, we'll be home soon, and you can warm up your bottom."

"Ethan, don't eat that, it's garbage." Daphne snatches a rotting cabbage leaf that was floating on the water away from her son.

"Aren't we supposed to eat those?" Ethan asks.

"Not if there are fresh minnows available. Don't be lazy."

"Em is catching all the minnows, so why can't I eat garbage?"

"For Christ's sake, here we go again, Daphne. You let Em steal Ethan's minnows, and you say it's all right. You coddle Ethan because he says his bottom is cold, but won't let him have a perfectly fine rotten cabbage leaf. You are giving him mixed messages, turning her into a chicken hawk and him into a turtledove. I thought we were finished with this gender neutral nonsense."

"I'm not going to be any Neanderthal's damn pigeon."

"That's enough out of you, young lady! No television for you either, Em!" Zachary is angry.

"Call it gender neutral or anything else you want, they both have to learn how to adapt to their new roles. It's up to them to choose where they are most comfortable."

"And what exactly is our job, Daffy?"

"Not in front of the children," Daphne says as she slaps the cold water vigorously with her wet wings, splashing Zachary.

《《《《〇》》》》

The Pettersens are visiting the Warren family and ring the front door bell. They wait a minute, ring the bell again, and then knock loudly. "That's odd, both cars are in the driveway."

Dr. Pettersen is holding Zachary's present, a five-CD set of Vivaldi concertos. They decided it wasn't yet time to spend any real money on their son-in-law, and bought him a token gift to show their good will. They are still very uncomfortable in his presence, and Mildred doesn't trust him.

"Perhaps they're around the back. Oh look, Lars, Emma does such a good job clearing the snow. Daphne told me it was now her chore to shovel and use the snow-blower. She loves to run the machine. That girl is going to accomplish great things, I can sense it."

The Pettersens walk around the side of house, then to the back deck, but don't see any members of the family. What they *do* see is four seagulls: two large ones, a medium-sized one, and a small one. They are sitting on the railing cawing loudly at each other.

"I don't know why Zachary feeds them. Now they're crapping all over the deck."

Linda Randazzo's Nut Tart Recipe
(as amended by Daphne Warren)

stry: 1 cup flour
¼ pound butter
¼ pound cream cheese
Cream together above ingredients, roll into small balls about
1" in diameter, and press into mini muffin cups. Makes
about 24. Chill while making filling.

ling: ¾ cup brown sugar (light or dark)
3 tablespoons beaten egg
2 teaspoons butter
1 tablespoon Amaretto liqueur
pinch of salt
¾ cup chopped almonds

Mix together and fill muffin cups with mixture. Bake at 350
degrees for 25 to 30 minutes, or until dough is slightly
browned. Let cool in pan for no longer than 15 minutes, or
tarts may stick to pans. Remove from pan and mangiari.

Optional ingredients for hallucinogenic Nut Tarts:
3 grams doxazine crystals
4 grams methylthiazide powder
1 gram speedizone paste
3 grams mortrate granules
2 grams silphocane chips
Mix thoroughly and dissolve in warm Amaretto.

Joe Randazzo can fluently read, speak, and write in 117 different languages. He can play first chair on every instrument in a symphony orchestra. He has memorized, word for word, every online entry on Wikipedia. Mr. Randazzo can still run a hundred-meter dash in under seven seconds, and can give you the name and precise location of every visible star in the Milky Way Galaxy. He constantly annoys and chases his poor wife, Rita, who has had to lock herself in her closet on several occasions.

Joe Randazzo believes in the transformative power of love, and the rejuvenating effects of a truly fine pizza. He is the author of eight previous books. He and Rita live in South Burlington, Vermont.